Hit and Run

"OK then. Hit that number plate."
"That's my dad's car."
"So? Who cares? Go on. Dare you."
The fair boy seemed undecided. At last
he said, "Reckon I could hit that easy."
"Let's see you then."
"I will if you will."

Joan Phipson

Hit and Run

Methuen

First published in Great Britain 1986
by Methuen Children's Books
This Methuen Teens paperback edition first published 1989
by Methuen Children's Books
A Division of the Octopus Group Ltd
Michelin House, 81 Fulham Road, London SW3 6RB
Copyright © 1986 Joan Phipson
Printed in Great Britain by
Cox & Wyman Ltd, Reading

ISBN 0 416 13232 4

Hit and Run

Prologue

It had been a dry year and the showground was thick with dust, most of it hanging at shoulder height and partly obscuring the view into the ring. But it did not obscure the two boys of about twelve years old who were playing at the back of the cars in the reserved parking lot. Constable Gordon Sutton, new to the district and on duty until sundown, did not know either of them. They had been climbing on a small pile of stones and now stood, each with a stone in his hand, facing one another. Afterwards the constable found that he could remember one of them vividly — the bright expression on the boy's face, the small half-smile, the wide blue eyes, and the hair, a gold cap on a smallish head. The other boy, less vivid, he had not remembered clearly. Later on — too late — he found out their names. He was near enough to hear what they were saying.

"Go on. You couldn't hit an elephant."

"I could so."

"OK then. Hit that number plate."

"That's my dad's car."

"So? Who cares? Go on. Dare you."

The fair boy seemed undecided. At last he said, "Reckon I could hit that easy."

"Let's see you then."

"I will if you will."

Because the sun was reflecting on the rear window, neither of them had seen what the constable saw from where he stood; that the two front seats of the Mercedes were occupied. The two stones flew almost simultaneously. There was a clink as one of them hit the numberplate, and the horrible sound of shattering glass as the other went through the back window.

Both boys stood paralysed, so that when the car door was flung open and the big man stepped out it was too late to run. That one of the boys thought of it was clear when he made a sudden move and then, as the constable interpreted it, decided not to desert his friend, and moved closer to him instead.

With dreadful deliberation the big man walked towards them. He did not speak until he stood directly in front of them, and then it was obvious that he was very angry indeed. He spoke too quietly for the constable to hear what he said, but the very quietness seemed to emphasise the anger. The constable noticed with some surprise that the fair boy had gone very pale and seemed almost beyond speech. A question had been asked. For a moment neither boy said anything. Then the fair boy turned slightly and pointed to his friend. The big man promptly pulled a notebook and biro from his pocket and began writing notes as the boy — his son — spoke. The other boy's face had become very red and his eyes, widening every moment, were fixed with a kind of amazement on the fair boy.

The notebook was shut with a snap and put away and the

fair boy was motioned into the car. He got in without a word. As the big man turned to follow him, the other boy found his voice.

"I NEVER," he bellowed. Then he turned and ran.

The big man retired into the Mercedes once more, and Constable Sutton stood for a moment, wondering. He had seen who threw the stone. But the small incident seemed to be over and he thought it unlikely that anyone as well-heeled as the owner of the Mercedes would bother to take the matter further. He walked on, but for some reason, perhaps because he knew an injustice had been done, he did not forget.

It was some weeks later, when he had begun to know the people in the district rather better, and could put a name to many of them, that Constable Gordon Sutton heard the rest of the story. The big man's name was Fleming and he was an industrialist somewhere in the city. This bland, pleasant district was his playground. This was where he had his hobby farm and where, to some extent, he sank his profits. A good deal more money was spent on his property than was made off it, but in spite of spending lavishly he was not popular. The fair boy was his son, Roland. Not a bad kid, they said — always polite but inclined to be showy, always been given too much. He seemed to like being in the country better than his father did and usually spent the school holidays here.

The other boy belonged to a family called Cornish that had lived always in the district. They were a big family and there was not too much money to spare. When Gordon heard that the boy's father had had to pay for Mr Fleming's broken window he went to call on them. Mr Cornish, just back from work, came to the door. He looked surprised to find his visitor was a policeman.

"Afternoon, Constable. What've we done now?"

"Mr Cornish?" Gordon smiled. "Nothing that I know of. Just wanted to ask you something."

Mr Cornish stepped back. "Come in?"

"No thanks. Won't take a minute. That car window of Mr Fleming's you paid for —"

Mr Cornish frowned. "What now? He want something more from me?"

"No. Just thought I'd better tell you. I happened to be passing. I saw your boy and young Fleming. I saw them throw the stones."

"You did?" Mr Cornish looked hard into his face. "My boy reckons he never did it."

"He didn't, either. It was Fleming's boy's stone went through the glass."

"Young Roland swore it was my boy."

"Young Roland was scared stiff. I saw. I only heard the other day you had to pay for the window. Wondered if you wanted to do anything about it."

It was a long time before Mr Cornish spoke. He frowned and scratched his head and sighed. And kicked the gravel path with his boot. Then he looked up. "What's the use? Fellers like that always win in the end. They've got too many big guns."

Constable Sutton said quietly, "You paid a lot of money for that window. I know. Tom from the garage told me."

"I did too — just when I didn't have it. But still —" He thought for a long time and then said slowly, "It'd have to go to court?" It was a question.

"Maybe. It would depend on how Fleming saw it."

Mr Cornish shook his head. "I won't do it. It's not worth making an enemy of a man like that. I'll let it go. Thanks all the same." He held out his hand and for the first time he

8

smiled. "I always reckoned my boy was telling the truth. I'm glad to know for sure."

Gordon shook his hand. "As you like, Mr Cornish, but if you change your mind, I'm prepared to come forward."

He heard no more from Mr Cornish, but the incident stuck in his mind and whenever he happened to see young Roland about the town he remembered, and he thought again of the broken window and the price the Cornish family had had to pay. He wondered what sort of a man Fleming was. As for the boy, before the accident he had not looked particularly timid — cocky, rather, with all that money. And a smile a bit too easy. But that afternoon he had been more frightened of his father than a boy should be.

Chapter One

One fine spring morning in September when Roland was sixteen, the truck from the Fleming property, Ranelagh Park, pulled in to the biggest garage in the town. The two young garage hands, Bert and Bill, who had been buried to the waist under the bonnet of an old Ford car, straightened up and looked at it. Fleming vehicles were always worth a look. They saw three men in grease-stained jeans climb out from the cabin and they saw the boy jump down from the tray at the back. They noticed yet again and with irritation that he was a good looking boy, fair haired and bright eyed. And about their own age. Like the truck he got out of, he looked brand new, clean and expensive. He was smiling, and perhaps it was because the two at the old Ford saw the girl accountant looking at him through the window with blatant admiration that Bert said now, "The very latest job. They don't come dearer than that." There was a sour note in his voice.

"There are bigger ones," said Bill. "And I don't go much on the colour."

"Oh, there are *bigger* ones, and I don't go too much on the colour, either. But that one'll grow — bigger, brighter, but no better, shouldn't wonder." He stopped and then grinned suddenly. "I wasn't talking about the truck."

A slow smile came over Bill's face. "Young Fleming, ain't it?"

He nodded. "Comes up every holiday from his classy school. Don't seem to like it too well at the family mansion."

"What's he like?"

"You'll see. Half a tick."

Roland was strolling round the cars lined up waiting for service. He stopped at a small, bright red Ferrari. The other three men were already preparing to work on the truck. One of them went over to the boys.

"Boss here?" Bert jerked his thumb in the direction of the workshop. "OK. We'll take the truck in. He's expecting us." He walked over to Roland. "A couple of hours, eh? You be back here round about eleven thirty. Don't go and buy more than the truck'll carry." The boys at the Ford saw that he was smiling.

"See what I mean?" said Bert. "Wait." When the truck had disappeared into the workshop he said, "Eh, Roland —" They both stopped work now and waited.

Roland seemed reluctant to leave the Ferrari, but he was smiling as he walked over to them. "Hello," he said, and looked under the Ford's open bonnet. "You got a big job there?"

"Nothing we can't handle, mate. What about you? Like to give us a hand?" Perhaps it was his tone, or perhaps it was the curious expression on his face that caused Roland's smile to waver slightly.

But he said without apparent effort, "No thanks. I'd like

12

to. I like engines and things like that. But I've got shopping to do."

"I bet." The voice was muffled, for Bill had his head in among the nuts and bolts again.

Bert now said, "Saw you looking at that Ferrari. Fancy it, do you?"

For a moment Roland hesitated. Then he said, "Don't you?"

"We both do, don't we Bill?" Once more Bill emerged from under the bonnet. He watched Roland. It was not a particularly kind look. Bert went on, "Trouble is we can't afford it, can we, Bill? You can, mate. What's stopping you?"

The situation was now clear and Roland lost his smile. "My dad can — a couple of Ferraris if he wants them. I can't."

"Go on. Dad'll give you anything, won't he?" Perhaps Bert had penetrated some kind of defence, for Roland blinked suddenly and his eyes, no longer quite so bright, slid away from the two boys and stared, unseeing, into the morning sky. When he looked at them again he said — and they thought his teeth were clenched — "Dad'll give me anything. Lucky, aren't I? Not like you. I don't have to work, see?" He was getting his own back in the only way he knew.

They were both watching him now, and Bill said slowly, "Noticed you weren't the one driving that truck there. Don't you like driving? Maybe that's why you haven't asked your dad for a Ferrari. Even without a licence you could drive it about the place out there, couldn't you?"

"Or maybe Daddy won't let you drive, eh?"

For a moment Roland stood there, and slowly his face grew red. Then he said, "I'll show you." And he swung round and walked towards the Ferrari.

They could not have guessed what he was going to do, and they never thought of stopping him. So that when he climbed in behind the steering wheel and started the engine the time to stop him had already passed. They saw him look down for a minute, sorting out the gears. Then, jerkily, and at far too great a speed he backed out.

"Hey!" they shouted together, and sprang forward, and if they had not jumped quickly out of the way he would have sideswiped them as he passed. As it was, he swept round the outside petrol bowser, lurched on to the street and before they had moved at all was away with a roar that only Ferrari drivers could appreciate. They were still calling loudly for the men from the truck when he was already half a kilometre away, and out of sight.

Now that Roland was on his way, and at a speed he had little control over, the first rational thoughts he had had for the last ten minutes began to trickle through his overheated brain. Where was he going? Why had he done it? And, last but worst of all, what would his father say?

He was now in one of the side streets of the town, and it was lucky that the traffic was a good deal thinner than it had been in the main street. Even so, the street was not entirely empty. Ahead of him on the right was the park, to which at this time of day mothers were taking their toddlers and their babies in prams and strollers. Behind him, although in his confused state of mind he had not noticed it, was the police station, out of which a police car was just emerging. And one or two cars were passing on his right on the way to the supermarket. Watching them, and now collecting his thoughts, he did not notice the pedestrian crossing coming up ahead. He did not see the woman with the pram who had so confidently stepped out into the road along the striped white lines. His red Ferrari had scarcely been in sight when she stepped off the footpath and now, half way across, she heard the roar of his exhaust, looked up and saw the car bearing down on her and her pram. She screamed and started to run. And then Roland saw her. His foot could not find the brake, his hands clutched and jerked at the wheel — the Ferrari's tender steering device — and the car swerved to the right just as the pram reached the kerb. The woman swung round to pull it up to safety. But she was too late. Roland scarcely felt the bump, but out of the corner of his eye he saw the pram roll over the kerb, and saw a bundle of blankets, out of which stuck two fat legs, flying through the air.

He did not wait to see where it landed. He no longer needed the brake. Instead, he panicked, and thumped his foot hard on the accelerator. The Ferrari shot away down the street until the woman, her baby and the white-striped pedestrian crossing were out of sight. And out of mind. For now he began to tell himself it had not really happened. Or it had happened to somebody else. The farther he went the more sure he felt that it had not happened at all. His mind told him he could not let it happen. In no way could he possibly be involved in a thing like this. His life would go on as before. Horrible, unwelcome mental pictures slowly turned to thoughts, and it occurred to him now that he would not have been recognised. It was not his car. If he took it and hid it somewhere far away no one would ever know. The damning fact that both he and the Ferrari would be identified by the garage hands was for the time being blotted from his mind. He saw only the way of escape. And still, irrationally, he was telling himself it had not happened at all. He pushed the insistent mental picture to the back of his mind — quite out of sight. He began to breathe more slowly, though the nerves in his stomach were trembling still. He eased his foot off the accelerator and the car slowed to a less noticeable speed. Then he happened to look in the rear vision mirror.

Chapter Two

It was Constable Sutton who eased the police car out of the drive as Roland went past. The speed and sound of the Ferrari caught his attention at once and he pulled into the street fairly quickly. He thought he recognised that crown of fair hair in the driver's seat. He had not forgotten the Cornish boy. And Roland had remained in his mind as a kind of unfinished business. Without actually thinking it, the feeling came to him that now the time had come — that now it would be finished.

He would have had his eye on any car going at that speed, but this time it was different, and his attention was focussed on the Ferrari with total concentration. By the time he had turned his own car it was some way ahead, almost level with the pedestrian crossing. He saw the accident clearly as it happened. He saw the baby flying so startlingly through the air. And he saw the Ferrari accelerate and make off at even greater speed down the street.

For a minute he hesitated. He was concerned with the fate of the baby, but he was also concerned that the driver of the Ferrari was getting away, and he had not had time to memorise the number plate. For a few seconds he slowed down. Then he saw that a number of people, mainly other mothers in the park, had converged on the woman and her baby. Everything that could be done was being done, and there was a great urgency in him to catch young Fleming and bring him this time to book. He settled himself in his seat, pressed his foot down and shot away down the street.

He was still some way behind when Roland recognised the police car. He knew that it was following him. And once again he panicked. Two thoughts only filled his mind. One was that he must get away before he was recognised. The second was that even a police car could not catch the one he was driving. It was necessary to work out a route. If he got on to the highway a fast car would not be so noticeable. And he planned his way through the back streets of the town, out into the open paddocks and onto the big interstate highway. He took his corners at tyre-screaming speeds, and he tended to swerve all over the road. A better driver would have reached the highway in half the time, but he was lucky that the other vehicles he met on his way were able to avoid him so that when he reached it, he and his car and all the other drivers were still intact. But the police car had gained on him, and when he looked behind again it was much nearer than it had been. He was feeling more comfortable with the car now, and with increasing confidence he began to gather speed. It was a divided road and there were two lanes on each side. He got into the right hand lane and settled down to outdistance the police car. Except for a few semi-trailers in the left hand lane there was not much traffic. He did not have to worry too much about being hindered along the way. His mind began to work more rationally. One thing at a time. And the first thing was to lose the police car. He looked in the rear vision mirror as often as he looked ahead. Sometimes it fell back. Sometimes it seemed to be gaining. He was surprised at its turn of speed. He did not dare look at his speedometer — in fact he had not yet had time to locate it — but he knew the Ferrari was getting near its limit. Clearly, he was not going to be able to depend on speed alone.

He realised that his inexperience as a driver was against him, and he had some idea of the risk he was running because of it. For the moment he could see no alternative but to keep on. If he slowed down at all the police car would catch him up. He was on the edge of panic again by the time the highway turned left round a bluff of rock and for a short time the police car was out of sight. Before he saw it again he passed two side roads, one to the right and one to the left. He still knew the district pretty well and he tried to recall where and when the next side road would come. If he could turn off while the other car was out of sight, and particularly at a place where there was more than one road to choose from, he might be able to slip away unnoticed while the police car roared away down the highway to the next big turn, or even, seeing no sign of him and guessing his manoeuvre, turned up the wrong side road.

The highway still twisted around scrub-covered hills, and he remembered suddenly that a short distance ahead was a turning that he knew. It was a dirt road and it led deep into the hills and towards an almost inaccessible valley where he had once been taken for a picnic. Also he recalled that other roads led off the highway in the same area, leading to coastal towns. If he could get onto the dirt road without being seen he felt sure he could escape. The thick scrub that the side road led into would be ideal for hiding the car. Also — and he felt his spirits lift — if they did notice that he had turned off they would surely think he had headed for the coast down one of the surfaced roads. For the first time the immediate future looked bright and he began to believe that this was a game, that he would get away after all, and so win.

The corner he was waiting for was not far ahead, but he did not dare slow down. Instead, he watched carefully, and when he came to it and turned, he braked hard. The tyres screamed and the car skidded. He never knew how he pulled out of the skid, but he did it to the shriek and horns of outraged semi-trailers as he slid sideways between two of them in the left hand lane, wrenched at the wheel and found himself panting, trembling, but still right side up and travelling forward between tall trees along the dirt road. As soon as he felt the car settle into proper balance he looked in the rear vision mirror. The highway was no longer in sight. There was nothing now but the trees all round him and the dirt road winding through them. He took a deep breath, and suddenly he laughed.

*   *   *   *

Constable Gordon Sutton was beginning to doubt the wisdom of his action. He was fairly sure it was Roland at the wheel of the Ferrari, but he had no proof, not even the car's number. If he lost the car now he would never know, and with a father like Fleming it was possible that Roland, if it were he, would never be pinned down. Also, the Ferrari was travelling at an unlawful and dangerous pace, and it was plain to see that the driver did not have it under control. He knew that if he were not chasing it, it would not be travelling so fast. His first feeling of outrage had left him, and when it became clear that catching the Ferrari was going to take some time, he decided to alert the road patrol ahead.

He approached the corner round which the Ferrari had passed, took it in a more controlled way than the Ferrari had, and was faced with an empty right hand lane. He had expected to see it some distance in front of him, but was momentarily surprised it could have passed out of sight already. Then he realised that even the Ferrari in the hands of a temporary madman could not have been travelling quite so fast. His first thought, as Roland had foreseen, was that it had turned down one of the surfaced roads that led to the coast. Then, as he slowed down and eased his way in the left lane he saw a cloud of yellow dust where the only dirt road branched away and into the hills.

"Now I've got him." He said it aloud, and turned off on to the gravel.

It was a narrow, winding road and because of the dust that still hung in the air between the sheltering trees he could not see far ahead. But now he could afford to take his time and, like Roland before him, he let his nerves relax and began to think. His first thought was for the baby. He had small children himself and the sight of that small bundle, so violently dislodged, had affected him strongly. Momentarily he considered where his duty lay. The decision to chase a hit-run driver, no matter who he may have been, had been involuntary. Even so, he knew it was the right one. If he had stopped, there was nothing he could have done that could not be done equally well, if not better, by the people he had seen running to help. And he was not the only eye witness.

He drove cautiously on the treacherous gravel, still half blinded by dust, but knowing there was no need to hurry, for this road led nowhere but into the scrub. Now that his

21

capture seemed sure, Gordon began to consider Roland's situation. Caught red-handed, as the expression was, he could hardly expect too much help, even from such a father.

"Serve him right." Again he spoke aloud, but even as he said it, the picture of the small boy's beautiful, terrified face as the back window of the Mercedes was shattered, came into his mind. The terror would still be there, and at once he knew that Roland was running not just from the law, but from something more frightening. For one second his foot came off the accelerator and the car began to slow. Then his expression changed and he pressed his foot down again. Even if he had for that moment wished otherwise he could not now let Roland go.

Chapter Three

Roland drove quite slowly and the smell of warm eucalyptus leaves and the sound of the birds came in through the window he had now let down. The wheels crunched steadily and reassuringly on the soft surface. He let the breeze blow against his face. It was a gentle touch and a promise that all would be well. All *was* well. The morning was bright, he was free and he was driving the splendid car that had saved him. He was well, active and nothing had changed in his orderly, ordered life. Everything was as it had always been — and his father was far away in Sydney, out of reach.

The picture of the baby hurled from its pram, that he had seen out of the corner of his eye, came back to him. Had he really seen it? Had he imagined it? His mother always said he had too much imagination for his own good. He breathed in deeply. He had imagined it. He had made it up, with his vivid imagination, after seeing the woman and the pram. He was running away only because he had — borrowed — this car and the police car was after him. It was cowardice, really. Soon, when he had had his morning out, he would drive back and return it, bravely taking the consequences. Not such a bad crime after all. His father might never hear of it, and if he did it was possible he might think of it only as a high-spirited, youthful escapade. He looked for the car radio but could not find it. He began to sing to himself. He had a good ear and liked music, though he kept his liking from his father. It was quite a pleasant sound that he made.

The road was narrowing and becoming rougher. The occasional potholes were not easy to see in the flickering shadows of the leaves overhead. He avoided them when he could, and felt, as the kilometres peeled off behind him, that he was increasingly becoming master of his vehicle — a heady feeling at sixteen and without a licence. He turned a corner. A long, straight stretch lay ahead. He pressed down the accelerator very slightly and felt the car respond at once. He had not bothered to look in the rear vision mirror since he had turned off the highway, but now, two thirds of the way along the straight stretch he glanced into it. The cloud of dust that rose up behind him made it hard to see anything. He did not expect to see anything. But he had a feeling that something had moved dimly in the cloud. At first, still feeling secure and strangely content, he did not notice it particularly. He was not really conscious that he had looked again. This time it was emerging from the thickest of the dust. It was the cream-coloured bonnet of the police car.

Immediately his feeling of well-being evaporated. His singing stopped in mid phrase and sudden terror sent the adrenalin surging through his body. He clutched the wheel and thrust his foot down. The Ferrari shot forward. He did not know that the thickened dust of his sudden burst of speed forced Gordon to slow almost to walking pace. He only knew that he was still ahead as he reached the corner. The skid he did on the gravel should have warned him that driving here was different from driving on the highway. But he was beyond rational thought. He only thought of escape, and he sped down the narrow road, twisting between the trees as the road wound upward, into the hills. Perhaps it was the careful design of the Ferrari, or perhaps it was his new-found skill that kept him on the road for so long. Now and then, unable to avoid potholes at such a speed, he allowed the low-hung car to scrape its bottom along a rut in the road. Sometimes a rock, unseen in the dust, cracked with a jolt against the metal. Suddenly, piercing through the mists of euphoria came the truth — that he had known all along he had hit the pram and that he did see the baby hurled from it.

It was remarkable that he kept going as long as he did, but it was inevitable that sooner or later the end would come. And it came as he tried to take a corner on a sudden down turn. This time the skid was quite out of his control. He did all the wrong things. He stamped on the brake, twisted the wheel the wrong way and as the car slid sideways towards a culvert, he tried to change gear. The crash, as the car hit the tree and somersaulted into the small creek sent any further thought out of his head. It was the seat belt that saved him, and when he found out that he was unhurt, although upside down, he fumbled for the catch and freed himself. Getting out of the car was not easy, but the rear window was smashed and he managed to pull out enough pieces of glass to enable him to get through. His fingers were cut, and his back was scratched so that he could feel the wet, warm blood making his shirt cling to his back. But he had not forgotten the oncoming car and his only thought now was to get away, into the bush, and hide until the police car should go away. Dazed, shaken and disoriented, he clung to this thought, and no other penetrated his shocked brain.

He stood up, swaying for a moment so that he had to grab the still revolving back wheel. He staggered as the wheel pulled him forward, but it stopped revolving as he leaned against it. His head was still ringing, but he fancied he could hear the sound of the police car. Panic, combined with the half-numbed perceptions of his shocked body, drove him to action. He pushed himself away from the car and ran, staggering at first, in among the trees and the concealing undergrowth. He pushed his way through, scratched by low branches, tripping over ground-level creepers, at first oblivious of caution or direction, but putting as much distance as he could between himself and the wrecked Ferrari.

Then, as his failing wind at last slowed him down, more rational thoughts began to take the place of panic-driven impulses. The first thought was that he was making far too much noise. Now that his loud gasping for breath had settled to a quieter and slower rhythm he was aware of the quiet of the bush around him. There was no wind and now, at midday, there was little sound from the birds. His own progress had been marked by breaking branches, snapping twigs and the thud and scuffle of his feet against stones. If he was being followed there would be no trouble in locating his position. This thought almost made him stop breathing altogether. He listened, as quiet and still now as his surroundings. He could hear nothing. If he was being followed, his follower had remembered to make no noise. Next, he began to wonder in what direction he had been going, and in which direction lay escape and safety. So far his thoughts went no farther than this. He slipped noise-lessly behind the trunk and into the shadow of a big tree while he took thought.

He knew that somewhere here, among the hills, was the valley he had remembered. But in which direction? He seemed to recall climbing up a long way and then, sud-denly, the land falling away in a series of cliffs down to the green depths of the narrow, unexpected valley. There was a track down, not easy to find, but he retained a rough memory of its whereabouts, and if he could find that — it was fixed in his mind that if he could get to the valley he would be safe. He had the vaguest idea of his bearings and the sun, almost overhead, was no help. But he knew that he must go uphill. He stepped cautiously from behind the tree, looked backwards in the direction he had come for one whole minute, and then very quietly moved away up the slope, making use of every tree trunk and piece of scrub that would help conceal him from eyes that might be watch-ing, unseen, from lower down the hill.

Chapter Four

Gordon drove his car steadily along the winding road.
There was no hurry now, and he kept well behind the cloud
of dust. Because he was driving slowly he heard the crash
ahead and speeded up. At first he could see nothing
because of the dust. Then, after quite a short distance, the
road suddenly became clear of dust, and he realised it was
somewhere here that the Ferrari had left it. He was on the
culvert and remembered the downhill turn. It was not hard
to guess what had happened. He pulled to the side of the
road and got out. The dust was settling behind him.
Already in his official capacity he had visited a number of
accident sites. He was, in a way, accustomed to sights that
he would normally never wish to see. It was always necessary to distance one's self from the impact, and he tried to
do so now. But he had not yet achieved the toughness
necessary to be totally objective, and he could not stop his
heart beating faster than was comfortable. He was already
working out in his mind what he should do in a variety of
unpleasant events, when a flash of red caught his eye. He

saw the Ferrari upside down below the culvert, smelt the leaking petrol and ran towards it.

The blood on the back wheel from Roland's torn flesh was the first thing he saw, and though he had himself in hand he felt his stomach lurch. But so far there was no sign of fire. He saw the broken rear window, for the car was tipped forward on its bonnet, and bent down to peer through it. There was no sign of Roland inside and the sense of relief for a moment weakened all his muscles. The blood on the back wheel was explained. But the boy, though capable of movement, could still be injured. He knew what shock and a damaged skull could do. He looked round the car, on to the roadside, down into the little creek, but there was nothing to be seen. He walked slowly back to his own car, thinking. He pulled out his notebook, looked at his watch, and sat down behind the wheel while he called up on his radio to report. His final words were, "I think it's important to do this on my own and it may take some time. The scrub's pretty thick here. I don't want to hurry it. I'll report back when I've found the boy. I doubt if he's far away, and I may need an ambulance."

He locked his car, put the keys in his pocket and turned back on to the culvert. Here he hesitated, stopped, and then returned to the car. He unlocked the door again and reached inside for his torch. Then he went back to the Ferrari. At first it was not difficult to see where Roland had gone. He had left a trail of disturbed undergrowth, broken branches and snapped creepers, and here and there were spots of blood — not a great many, Gordon was pleased to note. So far he seemed to have been travelling along the side of the hill and Gordon would have expected him soon to turn downhill, where there was thicker cover and the likelihood of water. He came to the tree where Roland had stopped, and saw the smear of blood where he had leaned against it. Gordon, too, stopped by the tree, and he looked about and listened. But there was no sound and nothing on the ground to tell him which way Roland had gone from here. Gordon left the tree and walked in a slow semicircle round it, looking at his feet as he went. When he found nothing he set off downhill to follow the course of the creek. He walked quickly, thinking that Roland was very likely in no state to travel quickly himself, and it would not take long to overtake him. When he reached the creek he stopped again. The creek bed was damp here, and soon, lower down the hill, there would be a trickle of water. He thought that Roland would be wanting a drink by now. He looked for footmarks to the damp creek bed but found none. He stopped and sat on a rock, and for a long time he stayed motionless, listening. And as he listened he searched the small trees and bushes that grew along the creek for signs of movement. And he listened for the sounds of birds disturbed by an alien presence. Birds will always give away the presence and position of a stranger, just as they give away the most silent of waiting hawks. But this time the birds were silent and in the windless air no branches moved along the line of the creek.

It took Gordon a long time to decide to return to the tree. When he finally did, he was sure that Roland, for some reason of his own, had not gone downhill to the creek. It was mid-afternoon when he came to the tree again, and this time when he left it he headed upwards. He hurried now, for he wanted to reach the boy before dark. At first the going was easy. The slope was not too steep and the undergrowth presented no problems. But for this reason Roland, if he had passed this way, would have left no tracks if he were careful, and Gordon believed he was learning to be careful. He continued on, but he was no longer confident that he was going the right way.

After a time the slope became steeper and the scrub thicker. He began to push his way through. And it was now, for the first time, that he knew he was right. He began to see signs where branches had been pushed aside, where small plants had been broken and crushed, and once, on a small patch of bare earth, he saw a footmark. He was not the first to come this way this afternoon. Certainty gave him confidence and he stopped and drew breath. As he did so he heard the sound of birds somewhere near the crest of the nearest hill. A wagtail chattered angrily and a peewit was shrieking its alarm cry.

"I've got you, boy." Again he spoke aloud. But this time there was a relief in his tone that was not there before.

★   ★   ★   ★

Roland climbed on, confident at first that he had not been followed, knowing that he must reach the top of this series of scrub-covered hills. Only at the highest point would he find the cliffs that led to the valley. The cuts on his back were stiffening and he began to feel the pain of them as his muscles moved below the skin. Also, the scratches on his hands were stinging. The blood from them had been smeared over his face and the front of his shirt. He was looking less and less like his father's son. And, now that the effects of shock were making themselves felt, he began to feel deathly tired. The alternative to finding the valley fairly soon was to give himself up. Even if he could not find the constable here in the scrub, he could return to where he had left the Ferrari. It would have been discovered by the police by now. This would mean food and shelter and a bed for the hours of darkness. He stopped and drew breath. He even sat down. But as he settled himself on the log he saw himself being questioned, being told, perhaps, that the baby — the baby — For the first time he considered what might have happened to the baby. What if he had killed it? Murder? Manslaughter? Even now he did not think in human terms of the accident except where he himself was involved. If it were dead his father would have to know. Events would be taken out of his hands. His father and the police between them would deal with him — somehow. He stood up and the same fear that had sent him scorching along the highway because the police car was following sent him on again, overriding the pain in his back, the weariness running like a tide through his body.

He looked behind once, saw nothing and climbed on. The afternoon was growing old and soon the light would begin to go. Already the shadows were long between the tree trunks. He hardly noticed. His eyes were on the ground before him. He had almost forgotten about being silent. His head had begun to ache and the only thought it now contained was that he must get away. He must keep on, and the fear that drove him seemed to build up as his brain grew more tired.

*   *   *   *

Behind him Gordon found more and more traces of his progress and knew that it would not be long now. But he was more aware than Roland of the approaching night, and he began to wonder where the coming darkness would find them both.

Chapter Five

Roland came upon the fence quite unexpectedly. He had ceased to notice his surroundings and only knew that his way led uphill. When he hit the fence — literally, for he fell against it and had to grasp the wire with his hands to stop himself going head first on to the ground — he remembered suddenly that there had been a fence, and that it led to a gate, through which the track led down to the valley. The relief made him look up and take notice once more of where he was. There were trees and scrub, still on the other side of the fence, but he knew that now he was near the top, and that beyond those trees the land fell away. And he had the feeling suddenly of space and free air moving and of the sky a long way above paling and subtly changing colour as the sun's light was drawn from it.

All he had to do now was to follow the fence, and he knew in which direction to go. Hope gave him energy, not much, but enough — enough, he knew, to reach the gate and go down to the valley. Caution returned with revived energy and he looked round carefully before he continued.

A new cunning even made him go a short way in the wrong direction, making it clear by broken branches and footmarks beside the fence that he had gone that way. Then he returned, placing his feet carefully and disturbing nothing, and went on his way downhill to the left. And the fence was beside him to support and guide.

He did not care that the daylight was leaving the scrub. There was safety in darkness and he knew his way. As he had seen no sign of the police he even began to believe he had already made his escape. But the idea was still fixed in his mind that the valley meant safety, and he must get there. The birds, settling for the night, were making a great deal of noise so that he did not immediately hear the high, thin sound that came up the hill on the calm air. All he heard at first was the chattering of wagtails, the small chirruping of wrens and, from far away, two kookaburras laughing the night in together. Also, with increasing confidence, he was making more noise himself as he followed the downward line of the fence. As darkness thickened and the bird sounds died it came more clearly, and at last he heard it. At first he hardly noticed it, and when he did, he put it down to the first stirrings of the night wind. But it persisted, and as he went on it became louder. It was not the wind, and he stopped and listened and wondered. It was a wavering sound, rising and falling, and somehow it carried with it the depths of despair and grief. Roland half turned back because suddenly he was afraid. But he had taken only two steps when he knew that he was more afraid of what might be behind than of what was ahead. He turned again and went on. The sound grew louder, rising and falling, now and then stopping altogether and then beginning again. The fence was leading him now to the saddle between the hills where he remembered the gate and the track were. He forced himself forward, not caring now how much noise he was making. The gate was not far away and the wailing sound was quite near at hand. Perhaps if he reached the gate and went through, he would be safe from — whatever it was. He crashed on, and suddenly the sound stopped altogether. He found that the lack of it was almost more frightening than the sound itself. Where had it come from? And what was now, perhaps, moving towards him? He stopped dead and waited, clutching the fence as if it could protect him.

But as soon as he stopped, the wailing began again. Suddenly with enormous relief he laughed aloud. He knew now what it was. Somewhere not far away there was a dog in trouble. The howling of a tired dog in pain was what he had been hearing. He went on to the gate with confidence. He did not even wonder what a dog might be doing in that place at that time. He was not frightened of any dog.

The daylight had almost gone by the time he reached the gate. But there was still light enough for him to see what had happened. The dog — a blue cattle dog — was caught by one hind paw in the two top wires of the gate. It was hanging there, helpless, and from the state of its mouth and the scratches on the wire netting where its head hung, had clearly been there for some time. There were marks still visible on the track through the gate that showed that a herd of cattle had not so long ago passed that way, and the story was now clear. The dog had hung back for some reason as the cattle passed through and, jumping the gate after it had been closed, had missed its footing, twisting the two top wires as it went over and catching one hind foot. What was also clear to Roland was that the owner, whoever he might be, would come back to look for the dog at some time. The sooner Roland took himself off the better. He wanted to free the dog first. It was painful to him to see it hanging there in agony. It had seen him and its helpless, yellow eyes were fixed on him, wide open and pleading, or was it in fear? He could not tell, but it had nothing to fear from him. He stepped up to it and would have held it while he freed its leg, but suddenly and unexpectedly it snarled and snapped at him, and its teeth caught him by the wrist and he had to wrench free, tearing the skin until it bled.

At once he was furious. He had wanted to help it and it had bitten him. Too bad. It could stay there. Keeping away from its teeth he opened the gate, slipped through and closed it again. As he walked on down the hill he pulled out his handkerchief and wrapped it round his wrist. It was painful — sore and bruised — and he was full of righteous indignation. Just then the dog began to howl again. And again he felt the helpless despair in the sound. He stopped. The dog would hang there, probably until it died if its owner did not come quickly. He half turned now. He did not care to think about it dying in that way. Probably he was the only thing that stood between its living and dying. Not fair, he said to himself, to be put in this position. But now he turned and faced the gate again. He thought of the dog's owner. If he let the dog go and the dog went home, the owner would not come this way. He walked back to the gate.

This time he was sure the dog's eyes were pleading with him. But he took no chances. He hunted about in the half light for a short, strong stick, and when he found it he walked up to the dog again. When it snapped a second time he managed to get the stick between its jaws. Reluctantly he pulled the handkerchief off his wrist again and with it he tied the stick firmly to the dog's mouth. Then he put his arm round its ribs and lifted it. When the strain on the two wires relaxed he allowed the paw to slip out. He put the dog carefully on the ground, expecting it to run away, and wondered what its owner would think of the stick between its jaws. He had no intention of untying the stick.

But the dog did not run away. It tried for a moment to stand on its three uninjured legs and then sank to the ground. Its eyes remained fixed on him.

"Go on," he shouted. "Get along home."

The dog struggled to get on its feet again. He raised his foot to give it a kick to help it along. The last thing he needed now was a sick dog on his hands. But he never delivered the kick. Slowly he put down his foot.

"Go on," he said more gently. "Do try." Again the dog struggled, and this time it managed to get its two front feet out from under it. It half rose, but the muscles would not obey and once more it collapsed. This time it raised its head, looked full at him and whined.

"Oh lord," he said. "Oh lord." And he bent down and picked up the dog. "I'm not going to take you home," he said into its ear. "You'll have to come with me." He felt a gentle tap on his hip and realised that the dog had tried to wag its tail. He managed to shut the gate behind him and started off down the steep track to the valley. The last of the daylight had gone and he had to move slowly, feeling his way.

*   *   *   *

Gordon reached the fence just as the sun dipped behind the western hills. It was clear that Roland had come before him, and it was equally clear that he had made his way down the fence to the right. Gordon followed the fence until the signs of Roland's progress ceased. He looked about for him then among the bushes and tussocks that covered the ground. He expected to find a sleeping, or unconscious body. He was tired himself, and Roland must now be on the point of collapse. But there was no sign of a body and the trail went no farther. It was not going to be as easy as he thought, and he felt the first stirring of a kind of respect for the boy. He turned back and began to follow the fence in the other direction. He moved cautiously and slowly, looking about as he went; Roland would have tried to hide himself when he decided he could go no farther. So that it had been quite dark for some time when he finally reached the gate. He could no longer see signs on the ground and there was no way of telling if the boy had continued to follow the fence, had gone through the gate, or had followed the track that must be there on both sides of the gate, back in the direction he had come from. There were too many possibilities and the light of his torch was not adequate to explore them all. There was too much thick scrub. He considered returning to his car to report. But he knew that after what he had said no action would be taken for the present. And he found himself reluctant to put any more distance than necessary between himself and the boy. He sighed and knew that he must wait until morning. Finding what seemed to be a soft, sheltered piece of ground, he loosened his collar, lay down and hoped that sleep would come. It would be a long night otherwise.

*   *   *   *

No night is ever totally dark and Roland made his way down the track. There was still no wind and the bush was very quiet. He was somehow aware that the hills were closing in about him, and when he looked up it was only directly overhead that he could see stars between the branches of the trees. The dog was motionless now, and warm against his chest. But it was growing heavier. He knew that soon he would have to stop. He had begun to stumble too frequently and each step took conscious thought. He did not even ask himself why he did not put the dog down and go on more easily. The decision seemed already to have been made. It had, in fact, made itself. He went on, more and more slowly, until in the total silence he could hear very faintly the sound of running water. He knew then that he had almost reached the valley floor. The relief relaxed the nerves that had kept him going. He stepped off the track and sank down, and laid the dog carefully beside him. He was more than half asleep when he felt it crawl close and settle itself against his stomach. It whimpered slightly and, still half asleep, he stirred himself, felt for its muzzle and fumbled until he untied the handkerchief. He felt it lick his hand as he drifted into total oblivion. That night his sleep was sounder and much longer than Gordon's.

★　　★　　★　　★

Gordon, in fact, had been lying awake for an hour or more by the time the first bird called. He was cold and something was pricking the small of his back. It seemed to have been pricking him most of the night. He watched as the night slackened its hold on the bush, and he saw the first faint outlines of the tree trunks emerge like the ghosts of tall men from the shadows. When the birds were in full voice he got up. He was stiff and all his muscles seemed to ache. In the first, cold, shadowless daylight he began to hunt for signs of Roland's progress. He did not have to hunt for long. The marks of his feet superimposed on the cattle tracks by the gate told Gordon clearly enough which way he had gone. He was puzzled by the marks on the gate and by the smears of blood he saw here and there. But he knew it would not be long now before he found the answer. He went through the gate, shutting it behind him, and started off down the track. He could see the valley below him now, and the cliffs that rose up sheer and jagged on its far side. Far below there was a small river and there was a narrow strip of open grassland on each side of it. In the light of the day he could understand why Roland had chosen this spot to hide, if he had known of it before. If he had not decided to follow when he did, Roland might have survived down in this secret place for some time.

As he went down the track the sun came up and the air in the valley was a fine gold. Light flooded the bush and the sky above. For a moment he forgot why he was here, and only thought, "One day I'll bring Mary and the kids here for a picnic." He hoped they had thought at the station to tell his wife he would probably not be home. He hoped they had told her he was in no danger. Sometimes he worried that she should be a policeman's wife. He had tried to explain before they were married and he knew she had understood. He was humbly grateful it had not made any difference. Now, with two little children, he considered they lived as happy a life as most, and happier than many. He thought of Roland, and knew that he would not want Roland's life for his own children.

He had almost reached the valley floor when he saw Roland. He was not hard to see. He was lying totally relaxed in the full blaze of the morning sun. There was blood on his face, and for a moment Gordon wondered if he might be dead. He was surprised to see the blue-roan cattle dog curled up beside him. Before he had time to wonder how it came to be there, the dog suddenly lifted its head and growled, then barked loudly.

Chapter Six

Roland's first thought on that warm, sunny morning was that he had forgotten to tie up his dog when he went to bed. He wondered how it had got into his bedroom. If his father heard it — Suddenly he opened his eyes. He lay quite still, warm, reluctant to move, wondering why there should be trees and sky above his head. Then he felt a movement against his ribs, touched with his hand the warm body of the dog and remembered where he was. As he tried to move he saw Gordon standing on the track beside him. He struggled to get up, yelped as his overstretched muscles and the cuts on his back protested, and sank back. He was helpless and he knew it, and his eyes, wide with fear and pleading, fixed themselves on Gordon.

"What on earth are you doing with that dog?" The relief of finding the boy alive and apparently whole almost overwhelmed Gordon. He hardly knew that he had asked the question. He saw the frightened eyes close for a moment in relief, and did not know he had spoken so gently.

"I — I found it — hanging on the gate. It couldn't walk."

Roland stopped. Apparently this was reason enough that the dog should be lying beside him far from the gate and at the brink of the valley. Before Gordon had decided what to say next Roland frowned and the dried blood cracked along his forehead. "I'm thirsty. I'm terribly thirsty." He said it accusingly as if it were Gordon's fault. The dog moved and whined, and he put his hand on its head. "I expect the dog's thirsty, too."

Immediately Gordon felt guilty. He should have remembered they would both be thirsty. Then his feelings lurched to equilibrium. "That's not my fault."

"Can you get us some water?" Roland had learned to know when he had the upper hand. So far the significance of Gordon's uniformed figure had scarcely penetrated his confused mind. Habit made him ask for what he wanted, and he expected to get it.

Gordon glanced down the track to the green valley and to the trees along the course of the river. "Can you get up?"

Roland made an effort to move, winced and sank back. "No," he said firmly. Then he added, "The dog can't walk, either."

"Try it," said Gordon.

Roland looked surprised, but he raised himself and succeeded in lifting the dog to its feet. It wavered, but this time it managed to stay firm on its three good legs. The fourth was swollen and obviously painful and it did not put it to the ground. The dog took a few unbalanced steps forward.

"See?" said Gordon. "The dog can."

"Well I can't." Roland lay down again.

It was the almost complacent expression on his filthy face that made Gordon say, suddenly angry, "Then you'll have to go without. I can't bring water this far. I've nothing to carry it in."

43

There was a silence. The dog took a few more steps forward. Its ears were cocked now, and it was looking down the track towards the valley and the river. The splash and trickle of water was just audible. Hesitant, wavering, it took step after step in the direction of the water. Roland watched it go.

Suddenly he shouted, "I carried it. I rescued it and carried it all this way. Now it leaves me." Almost, it seemed as if he were going to burst into tears.

Gordon looked down at him. "Trouble is the dog's got more guts than you have."

Very slowly, very cautiously, Roland began to move. He had managed to raise himself sufficiently to lift the dog. Now he sat up and put one palm on the ground. He tried to heave himself, pulling one leg beneath him. The knee gave way and he grunted and let himself down again. He did not look at Gordon. He tried again, and this time leaned over so that both hands were on the ground. He was on all fours now. And now Gordon stepped forward.

"I'll give you a hand," he said.

At first it seemed that Roland would shrink away. But in the end he nodded, and Gordon put his arms round the boy's waist and got him somehow to his feet. When it seemed that Roland had his balance he let him go and stood back.

"Now let's see you walk." And he put a hand under Roland's elbow. Slowly they went forward together. Roland made no more complaints, but little beads of sweat glistened on his forehead.

By now the dog had disappeared among the trees. It was not very far to the river, but it took them a long time to reach it. The final strip of flat green turf seemed to take longest of all. Neither of them spoke as they went in among the trees and saw the water moving at their feet. Roland shook himself free, fell on his knees and plunged his head into the stream. Gordon, after watching him for a moment, did the same.

The cold water going down his throat was a luxury greater than anything Roland had ever experienced. He took great gulps, and could feel it — cooling and restoring — making his body once again into what it had been before. Life came back into his nerves and muscles, and into his mind as well. And when he sat back, his face dripping and the water running pink off his chin, he saw Gordon as if he were seeing him for the first time, took in at last the significance of the uniform and knew that there was a future that would be neither pleasant nor peaceful. For the first time since he woke he wished he were here alone to battle with his thirst and hunger and aches and pains as best he could without help from anyone.

Gordon was standing up, wiping his face. Looking down at Roland he said, "Now wash the blood off your face and let's see the damage."

Roland was about to obey when he stopped and drew back from the water. "You can't tell me what to do."

"I can, you know. And you're going to do it. You're still a hit-run driver and you may have killed a child." As the memory came back to him he spoke more harshly than he had intended. He saw Roland wince and shrink suddenly as if he had been hit, and less harshly he said, "Why did you do it? Why didn't you stop?" He knew the answer, but to get Roland to admit it might be a small step towards salvation.

For some time Roland made no answer at all. But he bent forward again, scooped up water between his hands and washed his face. The bites on his wrist were stiff and

45

they stung as the water went over them. He fumbled for his handkerchief and then remembered it had been round the dog's muzzle. He found that Gordon was holding out his own. He took it without thanks and wiped his face and his wrist, which had begun to bleed again. Then, carefully, he washed the handkerchief in the river, squeezed it and handed it back.

At last, when there was nothing else to do, he said, "I was scared."

Gordon only nodded. "Right," he said after pocketing the damp handkerchief. "Let's have a look at you." He squatted down and looked first at Roland's back. Once or twice he gently plucked at the shirt, still stuck fast. "You did that getting out of the back window of the Ferrari."

It was a statement, and Roland only said, "It hurts."

"Not surprised. But I think we'll leave the shirt where it is. We could soak it off, but it'd only start the bleeding again. Just hope they're not too deep. I don't think they can be, or you'd have lost too much blood."

When he looked at the wrist Roland said, "The dog bit me."

"Naturally, if it was caught in the wire. They always do." He looked curiously at Roland. "You went on freeing it, even if it bit you?" Roland explained about the stick and he nodded. "Sensible," was all he said. "Anyway, where is the dog?" They had drawn back from the river and the inspection was over.

"He left me. He went and left me soon as he could walk."

"Don't forget he would have been even thirstier than you were. And, look, he hasn't exactly deserted you." Gordon pointed to a small rock on the edge of the water a short way downstream. The dog was lying on top of it in the sun and its eyes were on Roland.

"It's been watching you all the time. See if it'll come up to you and we'll have a look at it, too. Dare say you can stop it biting me." For the first time he smiled a little as he looked at Roland.

The relief of seeing the dog sitting there, watching him, was enormous and somehow unexpected. The relief that it was still alive and more or less well was unexpected too.

"Here, boy. Here." He snapped his fingers.

The dog cocked its ears, whined and slowly got to its feet. Unsteadily it stepped off the rock, and unsteadily it walked towards him. When it reached him it flopped down and its tail beat a very small tattoo on the ground. He put his hand on its head and looked round at Gordon.

"See?" he said. "It does know me."

It was not the time for congratulations, and Gordon said without expression, "Right. Now hold its head while I have a look at the leg. Be careful. It may know you, but it'll still bite if I hurt it." He expected Roland to reach for a stick as he had done before, but he only nodded and closed his hands round the muzzle.

The dog jerked once or twice in Roland's hands and whined once but made no worse protest. Gordon released the paw and said, "It'll be OK. Given time. Twisted and strained, I'd say, but nothing broken. Question is, what are you going to do with it?"

It seemed that the dog had become Roland's responsibility. He found the idea curiously satisfying. He said with more confidence than he had perhaps ever felt before, "I suppose I'll have to carry it up the hill again."

"I see. You'll find the owner and give it back?" There was no expression on Gordon's face.

"I hadn't thought. Suppose so." He shivered suddenly and looked upward. "The sun's gone. I'm cold."

Chapter Seven

They had not noticed, intent on the dog, that the western sky, high above the cliffs that ringed the head of the valley, was obscured now and a mountain range of heavy grey clouds was rising above the cliffs. Heralding them and floating lazily on the dying breeze one or two white wisps of cloud came low over the valley. The day had become still, shadowless and strangely warm.

"There's rain coming." Gordon stood up. "Have you had enough to drink?"

"What are you going to do?" Conveniently and inevitably the true situation — that here was a policeman and he was a prisoner — had been pushed to the back of his mind.

"What do you think? I'm going to take you back."

"And then? What happens then?" He began to picture the consequences of his return and his eyes showed signs of panic.

"Depends." Suddenly Gordon's voice changed tone as to him, too, the full significance of the last twenty-four hours returned. "It depends whether the baby lived or died. Neither of us knows, do we? Get up." The last words were an order, rapped out.

"I think I want another drink." Roland drank slowly while Gordon waited. When he had carried the dog to the water as well and pushed its reluctant nose into the river Gordon said, "Get up. Pick up the dog if you want to. We've got to get out of this valley."

Roland, still on all fours, looked up. Gordon was standing over him, his uniform now covered with dust and the cap pushed back so that wisps of black hair fell over his forehead. And Gordon's normally calm expression had somehow changed. Perhaps it was the night's growth of black beard. Perhaps it was the unusually hard stare of the eyes, or the jaw thrust forward more aggressively than usual. Whatever the reason it was not now the friendly figure that had so recently examined the dog's paw.

Roland got to his feet. He said in the tone he usually kept for his father, "I'll never get up that hill again — all that way."

"What do you propose to do? Starve to death here?"

"I thought you might —"

"I bet you did. You're not going to get off so easily this time."

The atmosphere, recently so relaxed and almost benign, had changed as the day had changed. There was little comfort in the air now. "What do you mean?" said Roland.

Gordon's momentary sense of outrage had passed. But he said, "I think you have spent your life sheltering behind your father —"

"That's not true. I —" The words were shouted, as if they had suddenly exploded out of him. But Gordon made a brief, sharp sound and held up his hand. Roland's mouth slowly closed.

"I know well enough that your father frightens you. But you expect him to get you out of trouble. I don't yet know why you were driving that Ferrari. I think it belongs to a man in the town. But I'll bet you had it in the back of your mind that, whatever happened after you — took it, that Dad would fix it. It's time you grew up, I think. It's time you took over your own life."

If Roland had been allowed to feel, if only for a short time, that this policeman was also a friend, he now changed his mind abruptly. His body, weakened by the accident, and undermined by lack of food, was rapidly losing its resilience. His emotions, never under sufficient control, now defeated him altogether. "You mind your own business," he shouted. "I was going to take the rotten Ferrari back anyhow. Do you think I meant to hit the beastly baby? If you hadn't decided to chase me —" he stopped, remembering he had begun to run away before he saw the police car. But he attacked now on a line of his own. "Anyway, you didn't stop to find out what happened, did you? You were too keen on hounding me. Just wait till my dad hears how I was victimised." It was a splendid word, often on the lips of television reporters, and he was glad he had thought of it now. Rage still carried him over his fear and a long way beyond discretion. Now that he was committed, he almost began to enjoy himself. It was as if something held back for too long was now being released. "You think you can do anything, just because you've got a uniform on. My dad could eat three of you cops for breakfast. He knows pretty high up people in your job. He'll soon fix you." As suddenly as it had come, his rage drained away. He stood trembling, red-faced, suddenly tongue-tied.

Gordon, who had stood impassive while the torrent of words poured over him, said, "Now that you've got all that off your chest, just pick up the dog — if you still want to take it — and start off up the track. I'll be right behind you."

There was one small kick left in Roland and he said, "Suppose you think I'll leave the thing to starve. Just what you would think."

"I'm not arresting the dog. Only you. Go on. Get going."

They started up the track. All words between them were spent, and the only sounds in the valley now were the splash of water and spasmodic, almost secret rustle of leaves in a small wind that began to develop as the cloud-bank covered the sky. Before long the rain started to fall, not heavy, but very constant. Overhead leaves began to drip and the dust on the track underfoot turned to fine yellow mud and their feet began to slip. They went slowly, for Roland carried the dog and his muscles ached with every step. His mood had changed. He would not speak again. He would not relinquish the dog. He would not give up. He would, ultimately, get the better of the man behind him. Once more the escape was into unreality, but this time in his mind, or perhaps in his body, there was a tightening of fibre.

Gordon, walking more slowly than he wished, fell back on training. He knew what he had to do and he was doing it. He was not obliged to feel anger or pity. He was not expected to decide right or wrong. There was a job to do and all that mattered was that he was doing it. He was almost as tired as Roland, and as hungry, but his physical condition was beside the point. For the present his mind was blank. When the rain began he stopped and looked back. Mist had come down now at the head of the valley. The cliffs were hidden behind the moving, flowing curtain of grey. Sounds, once sharp, coming up from the valley floor, were hushed. The birds had ceased to sing. He turned again to continue and almost bumped into Roland's back.

"Go on," he said. "Don't stop."

Without a word Roland began to walk again. Gordon noticed that his shoulders were bent, his arms pulled forward by the weight of the dog. The dried blood on the shirt was beginning to melt and run. Probably the cuts were hurting. The fair hair had sticks and leaves still attached here and there from the night's sleeping. Without warning a surge of pity swept the studied blank away. It was a boy still that walked in front of him, and he had been overtaken by events too big for him to cope with. He had not meant to do what he had done. Otherwise he would not now have chosen to burden himself with a dog whose injuries he could not be blamed for. Something had gone wrong with his life, and it was not his fault. A pity then, that this had to be the outcome, and Gordon himself the instrument. They were enemies now and there was no way out. By a logical progression he thought of his own small children, and wondered if Mary would be worried by his absence. His mind's eye suddenly filled with pictures of the small, domestic things of his own life, and he no longer watched his step, or Roland's step. Absently he wiped the rain from his face.

The track wound up the hill, now and then curving round a bluff of rock, or veering to avoid a tree that had been too big to push out of the way. The slope was steep and here and there little trickles of water began to pour out of the hillside, splash across the path and fall into rocky gullies already worn from the hillside by centuries of such trickles. The path was getting more slippery all the time. Like Gordon, Roland had ceased to watch his steps. Unlike

Gordon, he was no longer thinking of anything, but concentrating only on putting one foot in front of the other. The dog's weight had almost unbalanced him once or twice on the slippery track, but it did not occur to him to put it down. Inevitably a time came when his foot slipped on a rolling stone and when he tried to balance on the other foot, it slipped too, and he felt himself falling backwards and sideways over the edge of the track. With one hand he tried to clutch at whatever was in reach — at Gordon not far behind him.

Gordon was not prepared. He felt the hand thump suddenly at his shoulder just as he was himself off balance. If Roland had managed even then to catch hold of his jacket, though they would both have come down, there would have been nothing worse than muddied clothes and ruffled tempers. As it was, Gordon stepped sideways, found no firm ground beneath his foot and fell heavily into one of the little gullies below. He thudded on to the rocks, felt a sudden agonising pain in his leg and before he could stop himself let out a shout that echoed, sharp and sudden, through the clouded valley. He lay for a moment motionless, knowing that a movement would bring back the pain. Then, very cautiously he tried to find out what he had done. It did not take him long. The leg was twisted under him, bent over a rock in a way no leg should be. Even the slight movement brought the sweat out on his forehead and for a moment the day went black. He forced himself to take a breath, and opened his eyes.

The first thing he saw was Roland standing on the path above, looking down at him. Even now, in his own predicament and pain, he could see the exhaustion in the boy's face. But, also, it was a face from which all expression had been wiped. There was a streak of yellow mud down his side where he, too, had fallen, but he had not left the path and the dog was still, or again, in his arms. As their eyes met, Gordon heard him speak.

"I think you have broken your leg. Now I can get away." He sounded neither pleased nor sorry, but he settled the dog more comfortably in his arms, turned and went on up the track.

Gordon started to shout, had already drawn breath, but the sound never came. Begging was out of the question and useless. He lay, trying not to move, and watched the blood-stained back steadily putting more and more distance between itself and him. It was moving from him very slowly, but without hesitation. Presently it turned a corner and he could no longer see it, but he heard, or thought he heard, the slow, deliberate footsteps for some time afterwards. Then there was silence. The rain, still falling gently, made no noise. Even the small breeze had died. There was only the drip, drip of the leaves about him.

Chapter Eight

It is not easy to accept catastrophe fully and at once. For perhaps ten minutes Gordon half expected the boy to come back, and waited, avoiding movement of any kind, for something to happen. When, after ten minutes, nothing did, and the pain in his leg was still almost more than he could bear, he knew he was in great trouble. He did not — could not — pretend Roland would get help. The words, "Now I can get away", still seemed to hang about in the damp air. This was Roland's chance and he had known it from the moment he saw Gordon lying there with his leg under him. There would surely be a search party, but Gordon would probably not survive until they found him. For a time, something like total blackness settled on his mind so that he could not think at all. At the same time all power of movement deserted him. There was no way even of trying to ease the pain in his leg. This was despair and for the first time in his life he knew what it was.

In the end it passed, and he knew that he must deal somehow with the broken leg. Pain was only pain and could, no doubt, be mastered. He looked about for something within his reach that could be used as a splint. It was not only rain that glistened on his face as he began to move.

★   ★   ★   ★

As soon as he rounded the corner that put Gordon out of sight, Roland found that renewed energy had come from somewhere, driving his legs forward with less effort. He was going to be all right after all. A kind of excitement made him squeeze the dog so that it grunted and wriggled in his arms. He stopped.

"Can you walk?"

He put it down gently and noticed that for the first time it tested the ground with its injured paw. He took a few steps forward. "Come on," he said. "Can you?"

The dog looked up, wagged its tail briefly and began to go forward. Roland started walking again and noticed with pleasure that the dog was keeping up with him. It could not yet put all its weight on the paw, but was able to use it to keep its balance from time to time. At last, luck was flowing Roland's way, and in time everything would work out. He refused to think of obstacles like the wrecked Ferrari, or the police car that must have been left somewhere along the road. No one knew where he had gone except the cop he had left back there in the gully. Once he got home everything would work out. He might be scared of his father, but his faith in him was boundless.

Now that there was no one behind him, or anywhere in sight, and he was alone in the bush, there was no reason to force himself forward. He was already tired. When he saw a convenient log just beside the track he stopped and sat down. The dog came and sat at his feet against his leg. It began to lick the injured paw. Roland noticed that the swelling was diminishing. It was good to sit down. It was good to be alone. He moved a little on the log and the damp shirt pulled across his back. "Ouch!" he said, and the dog looked up. He did not move again, and the rain fell quietly but steadily on his head and shoulders and he felt it trickling down his back. His back had been uncomfortable all the way, but only now was he really conscious of the pain. It was bearable, but unpleasant.

Unexpectedly he thought of Gordon, who had not looked as if his pain were in any way bearable. He would be still lying there, and Roland wondered when he would try to move. The leg had looked horrible. Almost, he thought he had seen a piece of bone through the trouser leg. How did one move with a broken leg? He remembered snapping his arm once falling off a very small pony. They had told him it was nothing — only a greenstick fracture. But it had hurt. He remembered his father telling him not to cry — not to be a baby. But it had hurt quite badly and he wondered if his father had known how bad it was. The cop's break was much worse. Was the pain so much worse too? He got up, intending to go on again, intending to break the chain of unacceptable thoughts. Nothing moved at all in the bush round him. The path, looking suddenly very empty, very desolate, wound its way up the hill. The tree trunks in the misty rain had become quite black, their branches ghostly in the shadowless light. Without the breeze nothing moved at all, not even a leaf. In his mind the stillness, the lack of life, became a kind of threat. The comfort, the euphoria of a few minutes earlier had gone. He felt lonely, afraid, and once again fearful of what lay before. But also the thought of the cop would not leave his mind. He would be lying there still. And he had not called out. He had not asked Roland to come back. Why not? Roland was the only help there was. The pain would be dreadful. Remembering his greenstick fracture, he could hardly bear to think of it.

Reluctantly, and angry with himself, he turned and began to go down the track. Behind him the dog whined.

"You can go home, dog. You don't have to come." When he saw the dog begin to follow he only thought how foolish it was to give itself so much extra effort — with its damaged leg.

At first he could not find the place. He was almost back at the valley floor before he knew he had overshot his mark. Even now, when the cop must have seen him pass, there had been no call for help. He turned again and began to climb back up the hill. This time he recognised it and, looking over the edge of the track, knew why, this time at any rate, the cop had not called out. He had moved and was lying with his arm stretched out towards a fallen branch. The broken leg had moved too and had somehow twisted on the rock that broke it. Gordon was unconscious. It was at this moment that Roland had one of his rare practical thoughts. If he could get down there quickly he might be able to straighten the leg while the man was unconscious. He knew that it would have to be somehow straightened and splinted before there was any hope of moving him. He jumped down, winced as the jolt opened the cuts on his back, and plunged across the rocks to where Gordon lay. He took him beneath the arms and, using all his strength, pulled him away from the rocks. As soon as the movement threatened to disturb the broken leg he stopped. He could straighten it now, as Gordon was lying, so long as he remained unconscious. One quick movement before he came to would be all that could be managed. As if the man were sleeping, he let his body down gently to the soft, wet ground. He looked into the face, relaxed now, but showing signs of what the earlier movement had meant. Then he went to the leg. He felt sick as he looked at it, unnaturally twisted as it was. And there was a tear in the trouser leg, and something was coming through that he did not wish to see.

He put himself in the right position, reached down to grasp the black shoe — and then wondered if the right thing would be to take off the shoe first. But he could not do that without moving the leg. He clenched his teeth, took hold of the boot in both hands and pulled.

The howl that came from Gordon's throat almost made him drop the leg. He held on, keeping it straight. "I'm sorry," he shouted. "I'm sorry."

That one dreadful sound seemed to echo down the valley and hang about among the wet branches for a long time. But no more noise came from Gordon. When Roland looked up he saw blood trickling down his chin where the lip had been bitten through. His fingers were dug into the ground on either side of him.

"I had to," Roland said in answer to the accusing, helpless eyes. "I had to. I hoped you wouldn't come to. I'll have to splint it, you see."

He had never done such a thing before. He had never imagined he would have to. All the knowledge he had was from the brief first aid lessons they had had at school. Not for a moment had he seen himself in a position like this — where help was needed so desperately and there was no one to help but himself. He no longer asked himself why he was there, why he had returned. He saw now only the job to be done and himself, inadequately, to do it. He picked up the branch that Gordon had been trying to reach, found it more suitable than any other within sight, and laid it beside the leg. He tore off his shirt, grimacing silently as it came unstuck from the cuts on his back, and tore the shirt into strips. In the end he took his socks off too and used them as padding.

He worked carefully, steadily and very, very slowly, for he dared not make a mistake. He knew that every move he made caused more pain, but he heard no further sound from Gordon. Once or twice he looked up, and always found he was being stared at so fixedly that once he said, "I can't help it. I'm doing my best — trying not to hurt." He saw Gordon try to speak, but no words came and the grunt that he heard instead meant nothing except that the pain was bad.

At last it was finished. The splint was as firm as he could make it. The leg as nearly straight as the pain would allow. He sat back, wiped the rain off his face and looked to see how his cop had survived. This time the head had fallen back, the eyes had rolled up beneath the sockets, showing the whites below, and the damaged mouth had fallen open. At first he felt the shock of sudden fear, but then an unexpected spasm of anger caught him unawares as he thought, "If he's died and I did all that for nothing —" But he moved up and began to loosen the collar, undoing buttons that threatened to constrict the flow of air to the lungs. As he did so he felt movement. Gordon gasped, swallowed, and opened his eyes. This time he spoke.

"What are you doing?" He lifted his arm as if he would push away the hands that fumbled at his throat.

Roland sat back at once and said crossly, "I was trying to help." Then he saw intelligence come slowly into the fixed stare.

"I'm sorry. Thank you." It was barely a voice, but the words were clear enough.

Now that he appeared to be once more both conscious and rational, Roland said, "I thought if I splinted it you might be able to walk — to get out. Now I don't think you will. So what'll I do?" He felt the relief of being no longer the one to make the decisions. He also felt a great sense of injustice that he should have been put in this position at all.

He thought Gordon was not going to answer, for he had closed his eyes and looked as if he might have fallen asleep. Roland waited because there was nothing else to do, and after perhaps five minutes the eyes opened again and he was trying to speak. Roland had to lean forward to hear.

"You'll have to get help."

"Leave you, you mean?" Having come back to him it seemed an insane thing to do, now that he looked as if he might die at any moment. He saw Gordon take a deep breath and somehow gather himself. Then he spoke again.

"You've done all you can for me. Didn't know you'd come back. I couldn't — not such a bad kid — See, there was no — hurt too much —" He seemed to wander off.

Roland said sharply, "What do you want me to do?"

He said again, "You'll have to get help."

"How? How can I get help? I can't walk all the way back to town. It'd take too long. And the rain —" Bare to the waist, he was cold already, and sooner or later the rain would get through the blue uniform. In an hour or so the cop was going to be very uncomfortable indeed. Then he realised that even if he stayed there was little he could do. The rain would fall just the same. The leg would stiffen. And, he suddenly remembered, they were both extremely hungry. Cold and hunger and pain were three bad things.

"I'll go," he said loudly, so that the words would penetrate. "Can I get your car? Keys?"

It must have made sense to Gordon because he started to

fumble with his hand and then said, "Keys inside my jacket. Call them on the radio. Tell them —" He drifted off again, but in a moment said, "Can you use the radio?"

It was one thing Roland had learned to do on his father's heavy vehicles. It had been more to be able to boast that he could use it than for any practical purpose. But he could do it. "Call signs?" he said as he fished the keys from the pocket. As he did so he was pleased to discover that the cop still felt warm inside his clothes.

It took some time, asking the same question over and over again to get the information he needed, but he got it in the end. He stood up. "I'll be quick as I can. I don't know if I should —" But the cop had gone to sleep again — or something. Whatever it was, he wasn't hearing.

Clutching the keys, Roland climbed on to the path and began to walk back. He remembered the dog, but it had gone, and he came across it about half way up the hill. It was getting along, using the bad leg now and then, heading for home. It wagged its tail as he spoke to it, but kept on. He passed it, knowing he would not see it again, unless — he decided, no matter what the rules were he would leave the gate open. There was no reason why, because he had unhooked it from the gate and carried it so far, it should leave its proper owner for good. It was hungry. He had not fed it, and now that it could get along by itself it knew where food was. And he had enough to do now without looking after the dog as well. He was sensible enough to know there was no injustice, but it seemed as if there were, and undeniably he was saddened. To hell with the dog. He did not even know its name.

Chapter Nine

For a long time after Roland left, Gordon lay unmoving. The pain was easing, but exhaustion kept him half conscious. During the times he was conscious he tried to think. The boy had been back. He kept forgetting. But what he had done to the leg had been good, if more painful than he liked to remember. When he opened his eyes now, there was no one there, so he must have gone again. He felt very cold and wished the boy had left him a coat before he went. He only realised it was a silly thought when the picture of the boy's naked torso came back to him. Trying to work out why he should have been naked was too difficult. The only thought that kept recurring was that the boy had gone again. And the question he wanted answered was, would he come back? Beyond this he seemed unable to go. And after a time he slept more deeply, and dreamed he was at home and the children complained they were cold, and Mary said their coats had been lost and she was going to leave him, and the shock of that made him open his eyes. Without thinking he tried to move, and then his leg told him very sharply exactly where he was and why he was there. Before drifting off again he had time to remember that the boy had taken his keys and had gone to get help. It suddenly came to him very clearly that the boy could now take his car, ditch it somewhere miles away and no one would ever know that he was still here unable to move and alone.

*   *   *   *

The path up the hill seemed never to end. Every time it turned a corner Roland expected to find the gate. But it was never there. He began to wonder if he had passed through it without noticing. Several times he stopped and looked back, but there was no gate and the path disappeared round a bend. He would have stopped and gone back, but that he remembered the path had not led uphill on the other side of the gate, but across the hillside. The walking was keeping the worst of the cold away, but each step was getting harder to take. His legs ached and his empty stomach began crying for food, sending spasms of cramp through his gut that made him stop and bend over and pant even harder than he had before. He came to a sheltered place on the path, and there was an overhanging rock that offered protection from the rain, so he stopped and crawled under and sat down, bending forward to ease the pain in his stomach. When he stopped panting he noticed again the silence of the bush. The drip and patter of rain only emphasised the depth of silence. There seemed to be nothing living here but himself. Somewhere far below was the cop — and was he living still? — and somewhere behind on the path was the dog, still coming. But they might have dropped out of existence for all he felt their presence. He was alone — alone — alone. And he had never liked being alone. Also, he was alone with his problems and there was no one to help him. He was not used to being discarded and he began to feel as if he had somehow got himself into a nightmare. Even this thought was more reassuring than his real situation.

Now he told himself he would soon wake up. He would find himself in bed at the farm, with all his things round him, and Mrs Bates calling soon to say breakfast was ready. He would find the eiderdown had fallen off, and he would hurry to get to the bacon and eggs. The thought of bacon brought him back to reality with a jerk. He found, sitting there in this desolation of weeping trees, that his mouth was watering. A cloud of depression settled on him as he allowed himself for a moment to look into the future. There seemed nothing for him in it at all. Trouble was everywhere. His attempts to escape had been notable for their failure and, sitting there, he began to wonder why. The policeman — the policeman he had gone back to help — madness, and probably he wasn't so badly hurt after all. Could he still be there? Had it, indeed, ever happened? Roland might have retreated again into fantasy if he had not dug his cold hand into his pocket and felt the car keys. Reluctantly he returned to reality. He faced the fact that he was on his way to get help for a policeman who had been chasing him and who had broken his leg. He pulled out the keys and looked at them.

It was power that he held in his hand. These keys meant that he could enter the car, call up whoever — he could only call up the police headquarters, he guessed. But the key meant transport, mobility and the opportunity to get away offered to him practically on a plate. He felt his heart leap and suddenly the day did not look quite so dark. He even imagined he felt warmer. All he had to do was to get to the car and then leave it all behind. He decided to wait until he felt a bit more rested because there was no point in exhausting himself when he was going to need his wits about him. Perhaps he would not go to the farm after all. He had an aunt in Melbourne who had always been nice to him. From the haven of her house he could wait until his father had unravelled it all. He had no doubt that he would be able to drive the car, and a police car should have no trouble on the road. It did not occur to him that of all cars on the roads a police car was the most noticeable and the most noticed. As his legs ceased to ache and his breath came back he began to wonder why things had begun to look so black. There was daylight ahead after all, and it was not going to be so very difficult. He decided to wait another five minutes and then get going, and this time finally escape.

His stomach felt better for the rest, and he allowed himself to relax, determined not to let himself get so depressed again. A small noise on the path made him look up. The dog had caught him up and was now passing on. He called to it. It did not look up, but he saw its tail wave very slightly. It had known all the time that he was there. It was using the bad leg more often now, and it was going very slowly. But it did not stop, and it did not look up. After a time it was out of sight. For a long while he sat watching the turn in the track where it had disappeared. Somehow it had brought with it all the gloom he had just managed to get rid of, and what was worse, it had left it with him. The dog was on its way home. It had no problems except finding enough energy to reach the food it wanted.

He felt the keys again, and knew there was no escape for him. He would not be able to make himself do what he

wanted so much to do. He got up and stumbled as he stepped on to the track again. Hunching his naked shoulders
against the soft rain he began to climb. This time he delib-
erately put all thoughts but one out of his head. He concentrated on putting one foot in front of the other. He did not
pass the dog a second time, for its speed was increasing as
his was decreasing. But he came to the gate and shut it
behind him, knowing the dog was already on its way home.
After that the fence helped him and when he left it, the way
was downhill. He had thought he would have taken a
wrong turning at least once. But he found that his memory
of the route was almost photographic. He had taken such
care to go cautiously and to leave no trace.

He came to the tree where he had stopped, when he
realised he was making too much noise and too many
tracks. He remembered the care he had taken after that,
and suddenly he laughed. The sound, in the surrounding
quiet and stillness, was brief and shocking. If it had not
been for the dog he would have got away. He was sure of it,
and with all the energy he had left he hated the dog. He told
himself he could still get away, and this was why he was now
making for the police car. He had decided this as he sat
under the rock beside the path when the dog had passed
him by. But somewhere deep within him he knew it was not
true.

He went on, easily following his tracks now, and came at
last to the road and to the police car and the remains of the
wrecked Ferrari. The sight of that tangled red metal in the
ditch beside the culvert he found surprisingly painful, for
all that it seemed to him now that it had happened to someone else at a different time on a different planet.

The police car sat on the side of the road just beyond the
culvert. A few sticks and twigs had fallen on its roof and

bonnet, but otherwise it appeared undisturbed. He realised he had half expected to find a cop sitting in it, or standing by it. But there was nothing there at all. The road was as empty as when he had first driven along it. But now the dust was mud, and water glistened in the potholes. There were no wheel marks in the road. No one had passed this way since he and his cop had taken to the bush. He started to put his hand into his pocket for the keys, but found he was still clutching them in his hand. He walked up to the door. This was the car he had been so afraid of. This was the car he had tried so hard to get away from. Sitting here, wet, empty and covered with the detritus of the night it looked harmless enough. But he had to force himself to step up to it and slide the key into the lock.

The door opened like the door of any other car and he wondered, as he slipped inside, why it had been so difficult. He sank on to the seat and pulled the door shut. The interior of the car was not warm, but it was considerably warmer than the air outside, and it was dry and sheltering. He knew now how tired he was and he lay back, but sat up again with a gasp as the cuts on his back protested. As he sat up he looked round. There was a rug of sorts on the back seat. He was too tired to be surprised that it was apricot-coloured and had an embroidered lamb in one corner. He reached over and pulled it to him. Underneath it was a small pillow, also apricot-coloured and also with an embroidered lamb in one corner. He pulled that over too. Then he had a better thought, and got out of the car again and into the back. He was about to lie down when he caught sight of the radio on the dashboard. He knew at once how it would work, but now he was too tired. No one could expect him to do any more until he had had a rest. He put the pillow at one end of the seat, lay down and pulled the blanket over him. The relief was enormous and soon the warmth of the blanket began to quieten the trembling of his limbs. Almost before that happened he was asleep.

Chapter Ten

Gordon was asleep too. But he muttered and cried out as he slept. There were lines cut deep in his forehead, contracting towards the bridge of the nose — lines of pain that had not been there before. Now and then he made a movement, and these were the times when he cried out and half woke. But for the time being, and mercifully, exhaustion kept him sleeping.

He came fully to consciousness once during the afternoon when a branch, brittle after months of drought and weighed down now with water, suddenly broke and fell with a crash near his head. He felt the splash of water on his face and opened his eyes and, unthinking, tried to move. The immediate stab of pain cleared his mind. He managed to lift his head and look about him. He was alone and there was nothing here but the damp, dead leaves he lay on, the gaunt trunks of the trees and the grey-green of the drooping leaves above. For a moment he remembered clearly the events that had brought him here. And the boy had taken his car keys. He gave a kind of groan and his head fell back.

He was desperately cold and he wondered if he could much longer bear the pain in his leg. With the creeping cold the pain seemed to have returned after the temporary ease of the splint the boy had managed to attach.

Remembering then that the boy had once come back to help him brought the small hope that he might do so again. He recalled well enough that the plan had been for the boy to use his radio for help, but with the keys he had also handed him the opportunity to escape, this time probably with success. Running away from trouble, he guessed, was something the boy found all too easy. It was a risk that had had to be taken. He tried to move his arm to look at his watch, but found the effort too great. All feeling had gone from it. Instead, he let his head fall back again and looked upwards. The leaves were thick overhead, shutting out the sky, and little light was coming through them now. The tree trunks round him were losing their substance, becoming more like the shadows of trees long dead. And he was forced to face the fact that the day was coming to an end. The long night would come and he wondered if he would see the end of it — if he would see the daylight again. He thought of making the effort to move and to try climbing up out of the valley, of saving himself without help. But to do that would take more than courage. It would take a full stomach and a vitality he knew he no longer possessed.

He shut his eyes and tried to draw his mind away from his physical situation and to dive deep within himself, forgetting, if he could, the coming night, the increasing cold and his own body. But pictures of his wife and of his children and his home kept sliding themselves very clearly behind his closed eyes. Mary was at the stove, the children were at the table spilling milk or scattering cornflakes. The voices came too. "Johnny, *will* you sit still — Dinah, please wipe your mouth." And Mary's voice as he remembered it — high, gentle, but authoritative. It was these pictures now that took over his mind, so that he seemed to be there too, in the kitchen, the garden — with them still, in the ordered activities of their lives. And this time, as he sank again into a kind of sleep, the lines on his forehead were not so deep, nor so knotted.

★   ★   ★   ★

Roland slept for four hours without stirring or dreaming. It was only when he eventually turned over and the blanket slipped off that he woke because he was cold. It took him perhaps five minutes to realise where he was. When he did, he sat up so suddenly that the cuts on his back made their usual protest. With a deep sense of grievance he pulled the blanket round him. He looked out of the car window. The rain had changed to drifting mist. It must have been very thick mist because he could not see well at all. He realised with a shock that it was not the mist but the lack of daylight that made it hard to see. He looked at his watch, but he saw that the glass had been broken and it had stopped. He leaned over the front seat and found that the clock on the dashboard said six o'clock. At once he was overcome with horror. There was the radio, silent, and there, far away in the hills, the cop was still lying. And soon it would be dark. Not once did the escape he had so carefully planned come back into his head. All he felt now was guilt, and an unfamiliar and unpleasant sense of remorse. He knew what he had to do, and before he could persuade himself not to do it, he climbed through into the driver's seat. For a few minutes he studied the radio. Then he reached out his hand. He had to make an effort to stop it shaking.

72

Because of his own inexperience it took him some time to make contact. When he did — when he heard a brisk voice answer he could think of nothing to say. The voice at the other end became urgent, and finally he spoke. It took some time for the man at the other end to grasp his rambling explanation of who and where he was, and what had happened. When he did, the voice became more urgent still and he was told to stay where he was, to wait until they came and not to move from the police car, much less try to drive it away. "The end of the road'll be blocked before you can reach it," the voice said in no kindly tone. He cut out then, and sat back, ignoring the pressure on his cuts. His body felt better for the long sleep, but he was hungrier than ever. He found himself looking through the windscreen on to the wet, yellow road with its overhanging trees. It was becoming like a tunnel in the fading light. Without warning he thought again of the cop, still lying there, also in the fading light, uncovered, in the rain. For a long time he sat thinking of the cop, thinking of himself — thinking. Then he allowed himself one short, loud expletive, and began to investigate the interior of the car. He found no food, but he did find a thick parka and a mackintosh cape. He gathered these up, together with the apricot-coloured blanket with the embroidered lamb, and the small apricot-coloured pillow with the same embroidered lamb, and he opened the car door and climbed out. He left the ignition keys in the car because he forgot to take them out. He put on the parka and threw the cape round his shoulders. Then he gathered up the blanket and pillow, stuffed them under his arm and began again the long walk back to the valley. He went as quickly as he could, because he had to reach the fence before dark. After the fence he would be able to find his way. As he walked, and climbed he refused

73

to let himself think at all. Only once on the way did he ask himself why he was doing this. No satisfactory answer came to him, but he went on, angry and protesting.

Daylight had almost gone by the time he reached the fence. But the misty rain was clearing. With the parka, the cape and the energy required by the climb he was warm again. He began to think he would get to the cop after all. He put his hand on the fence and followed it down to the gate. Opening the gate and going through, he thought of the dog. He would not see it again. He would never know its name and he would never know where it belonged. But for a short time it had become part of his life, and if it had not been for him it would still be hanging on the gate. He found a certain satisfaction in the thought.

The downward track was just visible. He shut the gate and started down. In the gathering darkness his pace became slower and slower. It was not until he reached the level valley floor that he realised he had done it again. He had gone past his cop in the dark. He stopped to drink at the river, and cursed as one foot went into the water. It occurred to him that the cop would be thirsty, too, but he had nothing to carry water in. Perhaps he would be wet enough in the rain. It was a queer kind of joke. He turned and trudged back up the hill.

He had to shout before he found his cop. He shouted for a long time, as loudly as he could. In the silence of the night his voice was frightening. At last, when he had walked up and down the stretch of track several times he thought he heard an answer. He stopped and listened. The sound had stopped and he shouted once more. This time he heard it clearly. It was more of a moan than an answering shout, but he was able to locate it and he went as fast as he was able towards it.

The cop was lying exactly as he had left him, but now he was a good deal wetter. It was hard to see his face clearly, but it seemed to Roland that he had become rather suddenly an older man. His eyes were open and Roland knew they were fixed on him. The voice, when it came, was little more than a whisper.

"You came back."

Because he had so nearly not come back he was suddenly angry. "Naturally I came back. That's what I was to do, wasn't it?" This time he heard no reply. He knew the eyes were still fixed on him and he knew why. "So," he said and his voice was strangely aggressive. "I did what you said. I called them up. They're coming." The eyes closed then, and because the cop failed to ask why he had been so long, he found himself saying, "I went to sleep, see? Didn't mean to."

The cop spoke again. "Doesn't matter. You came." To his surprise he felt a touch on his arm, and found it was the cop's hand reaching out. He had been squatting down but now, suddenly embarrassed, he got up.

"Look. I found these in your car. Thought it might be warmer for you." He pulled the blanket from under his arm, shook it out and threw it over him. The pillow fell out of it and he picked it up and found himself saying absurdly, "Excuse me," as he lifted Gordon's head and slipped it under. He shook off the cape and slipped out of the parka and threw them both on top of the blanket, the cape protecting all from the rain. "Should be warmer," he said when he had finished. The cold struck sharply on his own bare back. He was glad the rain was easing. He squatted down and peered into the cop's face.

"What'll I do now?"

It was hard to believe the boy had come back. It was even

harder to believe he had done what he had been supposed to do, and that help would come. Gordon felt the weight of the blanket and the parka and was aware that his head was more comfortable. His brain took in this much. There were questions to be asked, but now he only knew there would be an end to this cold — this pain. It was only a matter of waiting. Some of the numbness was beginning to leave his body and with the first of the renewed warmth the vitality that had been flickering so low returned and it was as if he began to live again. He heard the boy's question and because he was not able to answer it he put one of his own.

"What's your name? I know it's Fleming. Your other name?"

"Roland. What's yours?"

"Gordon. Silly name."

"It's OK. So what'll I do now, Gordon?" Now that his cop began to show signs of recovery and because it was due to his own unaided efforts, he suddenly felt, like any housewife, that he must bustle about improving the situation. Besides, moving was warmer than sitting still.

This time the question registered. "Could you light a fire? Keep us warm. Show them where to come."

He would have tried, even with the sodden sticks and the wet bark. But there were no matches and nothing at all to light a fire with. Gordon was fully awake now, and Roland knew his eyes were peering into the darkness, trying to see him. They must have seen something, for Gordon said, "Where's your shirt? You're naked."

At once he felt guilty and began to excuse himself. "On the splint. See, I didn't have anything else. Was only an old shirt." He was sure that for the first time Gordon smiled. He caught the gleam of teeth through the scruffy black stubble.

76

Gordon said now, "You'll be cold. You are cold."

"Doesn't matter. Can't be helped. I was warm there for a bit, anyway." He thought Gordon was going to suggest putting on the parka and he'd be damned if he'd take it off him, now that it was doing such good work. He didn't fancy all that effort going for nothing.

But this was not what Gordon said. "You'd better get under the rug — whatever it is — with me. We'll keep each other warm until they come."

"I might hurt your leg."

"Come on the other side. And just be careful."

So he crawled in, sliding under the blanket and the parka and pulled them over him. Even now there was little warmth coming from his cop's body and he could feel that clammy wetness of the uniform against his chest. They lay for a time without speaking and little by little in spite of the wet uniform a kind of warmth began to flow between them. Roland did not dare move, but he felt Gordon wriggle his shoulder, and said, "OK?"

"Better every minute." The voice was not exactly powerful, but there was a ring to it that was not there before. "When do you think they'll be here?"

It was something Roland had been asking himself for some time. "They were coming straight away — said they'd be at the turning before I could get there if —" It was hard to go on.

Gordon went on for him. "If you decided to run off with my car?"

"They told me to wait till they came."

"Why didn't you? They'd want you to show them the way."

It seemed a silly question. He said, suddenly angry, "I couldn't, could I? With you down here. And I'd found the parka and the blanket." He stopped and then said, "Anyway, why do you keep pictures of lambs on your rugs? And on the pillow, too. Seems silly for a cop."

"They belong to my kids. Mary left them there by mistake."

"You've got kids?" It was the first time Roland had thought of his cop — any cop — as having a family of his own. Now he said, "What kids have you got then?"

Gordon told him. He described the two children, their ages, their looks, their personalities and his hopes for them in the future. He talked about his wife and their family life together. He found it good to talk about them. When he was finished, Roland was silent for so long that he said, "Now you tell me about yours."

Even then he was slow to start. When he did, he spoke reluctantly, as if his memories of home were not to be recalled with any particular pleasure. He began slowly. "Our home's not like yours. See, it's really in Sydney. But I like it here and Dad doesn't mind if I come. Easier for Mum, too. She's so busy. They never know what to do with me at home."

"What does she do, then?"

"Committees and things. She's very *good* — you know, working for sclerosis, the blind, women's refuges — I don't remember them all. But she's not home much. So it's better for me here. There's Mrs Bates who minds the house. She's always there, and there's plenty to do." He stopped. Then, as if aware suddenly that the picture he had drawn of his mother had done her less than justice, he added, "Mum cares about me and all that. It's just that her work is so important. She keeps saying if I really need her she'll always be there. It's just that, so far, I haven't — not as much as all those other things, anyway."

78

"I see." And he did see — more than he had before. The father too busy to do more than get him out of trouble when he got into it; the mother waiting for him to tell her when he needed her. Busy people. Perhaps simply blind people. He said carefully, "Do you remember a day at the show when you threw a stone through the back window of your father's car?"

Without thought Roland spoke quickly and loudly. "I never did."

"Well, you did, you see. I saw you. Wondered at the time why you blamed the other kid. Your own dad —"

Roland gave a kind of grunt and was silent for a long time. When he did speak his voice was quiet and very slow. "You'd never catch me telling you, only here we are, like this, and somehow it seems different. Dad's always telling me how silly I am and that, and he gets angry if he thinks I'm too silly." He stopped, and then said, suddenly loud, "I'm not silly. I get better marks at school than most."

"You're not silly. Go on."

"He gets angry, and — and I suppose he frightens me. His way of punishing is — like one day I'd done something he thought was silly and he made me tell the whole class what I'd done. He telephoned the teacher and said I was to."

"That wasn't very fair, was it?" Gordon was astonished, but he spoke mildly.

"Fair? Dad isn't all that keen on fair. I found that out when I was thirteen."

"Tell me."

Chapter Eleven

It was something Roland had told no one because at the time he had been ashamed and too confused to sort his thoughts out properly. Now in the dark and the silence, and the man beside him quiet, uncritical and interested, he told it. There was not really much to tell.

It was the end of the year examinations and the general science paper. He knew he had not done enough work for it and he was afraid of what his father would say — and do — if his marks were poor. He also knew that his father set great store by good marks, particularly in science. "It's the way to get on," he'd say. "Have something to show for yourself."

Ordinarily exams were no trouble for Roland and he always did reasonably well without trying very hard. But this time he knew there would be no hiding his lack of knowledge. The answers would be either right or wrong. He could not imagine, as he walked in and sat down for the science paper, why he had not worked harder for this particular exam. He was sweating and his hand was shaking even before he read the paper. He had only to glance through it to know he was in for trouble.

A big class was taking the examination and the boys were sitting closer together than was usual. So it was not beyond the bounds of possibility for one boy to see another's work and his answers to the questions. Desperate, not afraid of failing, but afraid of his father, Roland, not too skilfully, copied the answers from the boy next to him, who had a reputation for being a brain. He remembered still the moment later on when the master had called him to the staffroom, sat him down and told him, with the examination papers in front of him, that he had cheated.

"You see, when Alister went wrong, you went wrong in the same way. He didn't make many mistakes, and neither did you, but you made the same mistakes. I'm afraid there's no doubt."

In the face of this he could only grow scarlet and admit it. The worst moment was when the master said, "I'm afraid I'll have to tell your father."

He had burst out, "No! Please."

But there was no getting out of it. And the letter he was made to take home told everything.

"What did your father do?" said Gordon.

"That — see, that was the trouble. He was angry — oh, he was mad at me. He shouted. But afterwards when I was by myself and able to think, I realised it wasn't because I had cheated, and that's what I felt so ashamed about. It wasn't that at all. It was because I'd been found out. Do you know what he said? 'If you must cheat, cheat. If you decide to be dishonest, OK. But never let yourself be found out. Get on if you can without having to be dishonest, but, by God, if you have to, never let yourself be found out.'" He stopped speaking and for a long time thought Gordon was not going to say anything.

But then Gordon said very carefully, "I think your father was wrong, don't you?"

"How can he be? That's it, see? How can he be? Look how important he is. Look how much money he's made. I know he didn't have much to begin. And everyone thinks he's so marvellous. Do you know, they might make him a knight, even. He told me. And he was pleased. If he likes so much for people to think him good, he must think what he does is good. Mustn't he? Mustn't he?"

It was a question no tired cop with a compound fracture of the leg could be expected to answer on a black, wet night. But if he had no answer he now saw and understood a good deal he had not before. He did the best he could. "You know the worst trouble I have?"

"Wouldn't think you had any. Look at your home and the kids and all."

"It's not that. I mean — things you do when you're not, sort of watching. For a job like mine it's not too good."

"You cheat too?" Roland sounded so appalled, so utterly shaken that, even here, in these circumstances, Gordon laughed.

But he still spoke very carefully. "I didn't mean cheating particularly. I meant — well, see, there was this time ..."

He still remembered it so clearly, and imagined that he always would. He had not long finished his training. He was on his way home from a long day's work and seeing signs of some kind of scuffle at the far end of the street he was travelling, he speeded up. He had thought the sight of the police car approaching might have broken up whatever it was. But no one, it seemed, had noticed him come. They were all still there — a gang of children, quite small children, round something on the ground. They were shouting and laughing and at first it seemed they were simply getting rid of animal spirits bottled up during school hours. He had stopped the car and walked towards them. Then one of them saw him.

"Hey, cop!" he had shouted and they all broke away like a flock of sparrows from an upturned dustbin. Except that this was no dustbin. This, as he now saw, happened to be a man lying on the ground. So at once he reached out his arm and managed to gather in a couple of the kids as they ran past. Holding them fast, though they wriggled and kicked at his shins, he went to find out why such a large, comparatively young chap should have let himself be bowled over by kids, none of whom looked much older than ten.

"Lemme go. You're hurting," one of the kids howled in his ear. He only clutched them rather tighter, for the man, he saw, was bleeding at the mouth. As he watched, the man pulled himself up and dabbed at his face. And then Gordon recognised him. He was a slightly retarded fellow who lived with his mother somewhere in the neighbourhood. He was always on the streets, wandering up and down, and everybody knew him. "Bert," they called him and usually said hello when they passed. The kids must have known him, too, and known he was harmless and even, sometimes, kind, for everyone knew he was fond of kids. So why this?

Still hanging on to the children — one boy and one girl — he said, "What happened, Bert? What did they do?"

But Bert only smiled in a puzzled way and said, "Fell over — an' then the kids came. Didn't want them to kick me —"

"They kicked you?"

The boy under his arm now shouted, "I never. I never did it. Only his backside."

The girl now felt brave enough to add, "Anyway my mum says he shouldn't be allowed about the streets, not

83

when us kids is coming back from school. That's what I said to the others when we saw him fall over."

Gordon saw it all now. "So that's when you all went for him — before he'd had time to pick himself up?" Before he let them go he had shaken them till their teeth rattled. "You ever do that again you'll be in so much trouble you'll wonder what hit you. Now go home. And stay there."

They had run off without a word, and when he helped Bert to his feet he saw that he was not too much damaged. When he asked about his mouth Bert had said, "See, it was only a gym shoe. Kids didn't mean nothing. Just got a bit excited. Kids do."

Gordon had thought that was the end of the incident until he found himself on the mat because the girl's mother had complained that there had been bruises on the girl when she got home. She had even used the words Police Brutality.

"See, Roland, I was too rough with them. They were only silly kids and they hadn't actually pushed Bert over — only made the most of the opportunity when they saw him go down. I thought it had taught me a lesson. But I'm not sure. Sometimes I think I could do the same again."

When it was clear he had no more to tell, Roland said, "I don't call that so terrible. Expect I'd have done the same."

"You're not a policeman. The sergeant didn't think too much of it. If it happened again — You see I was making a judgement, which I'm not supposed to do. And I was making it without thinking. That's even worse." He did not know why he had decided to tell the boy this now. It was not going to help him with his father.

But it seemed that perhaps it had, for after a long silence Roland said, "It's ways of doing things, isn't it, really?"

"That, and the funny things everybody sometimes does

— like you and me being here under my kid's blanket — funny, that is."

And for the first time he heard the boy laugh.

Chapter Twelve

There was not much talk after that. They were both warmer, and if the broken leg still hurt there was no indication of it. Gordon kept it to himself. The rain had stopped and the mist seemed to be clearing. But the night had grown much colder. They were glad of each other and of the covering Roland had brought. They might have drifted into a kind of sleep, because it seemed very much later when Gordon said, "Shouldn't they be here by now? How long ago is it since you talked to them?"

There was no knowing. Gordon's watch, too, had been broken when he fell and there was nothing in the opaque darkness to tell them how the night progressed. But Roland said, "I did tell them how to get to the fence. They thought I'd be there to show them so perhaps they didn't listen. But after the fence it's easy. Just follow it to the gate and then down the track. They couldn't miss that."

"We'd better listen in case they call."

After that they lay awake and after a time Roland wriggled out and sat up. The sudden cold hit him unexpectedly and he gasped. But he made himself sit exposed and half frozen while he listened to any sound there might be. After what seemed a long time and after he began uncontrollably to shiver he slipped down again.

"Nothing," he said. "Not even a mopoke and it's cold as ice."

"You don't have to tell me," said Gordon. "I can feel you shivering." They continued to wait, alert now for any sound at all. At last from very far away there came something that might or might not have been a night bird's call. Roland sat up again. He waited, and the sound came again. "Better shout," said Gordon. "If it isn't them it doesn't matter."

So Roland filled his lungs and let out a long coo-ee. The silence that followed seemed to throw the sound back at him. They waited, holding their breath.

"Again," said Gordon. "Do it once more."

He coo-eed again, and this time some wakened bird in the high branches down in the valley squawked in protest. But there came an answering call from high up on the hillside where they had thought the first sound had come from.

"That's them," said Gordon. "They've heard you. They'll know to come on down now. We just wait and answer if they shout." If he felt relief that his long ordeal was at an end he gave no sign. Perhaps, in the comparative comfort and relief of having the boy beside him again he had forgotten the early period of acute pain and of despair. Perhaps he was thinking that now it would be Roland's turn, that now there would be no stopping what are called 'the due processes of the law'.

This thought was insistently in Roland's mind, and with brutal clearness the memory of the accident came back to him. For a long time he had managed to forget all about it.

In a few minutes, a quarter of an hour perhaps, he would be confronted with it. He said, with all his new confidence evaporated, "Gordon —"

To his surprise he felt Gordon's hand close on his wrist. It was warm and comforting. "I know. We'll find out now. There's nothing to do but wait." And the comfort of his hand was all the comfort there was. They listened in silence for the first sound of footsteps down the track. For a time they heard nothing, and while they waited Gordon said, "You know, don't you, that even if — supposing the baby was quite all right, you're still in quite bad trouble? I don't want you to pretend to yourself it'll be any different because you've done what you have for me. You know I'm grateful, but there's nothing I can do to stop what's going to happen. You do know that, don't you?"

"Yes," he said, and this time could not pretend it could be otherwise.

Gordon had not quite finished. "If it's any help to you, I'm pretty confident you'll stand up to — whatever happens. See, I know what you've stood up to already, even if you didn't really want to. And you didn't want to come back, did you?"

Roland said, "No," after a pause.

"It shows something about you that you made yourself do it, don't you think?"

With a sudden and uncharacteristic spurt of honesty Roland said, "I only came because it was uncomfortable for me, thinking of you down here with your busted leg and so wet and all. It was the same with the dog. I was uncomfortable having to think of it hanging there."

To his surprise Gordon laughed. "You're a queer chap, Roland. First you pretend nothing terrible's happened at all. Then you suddenly collect it all and wear it like a hair shirt." He ended mildly, "You want to keep to the middle if you can."

The unexpected sound of his laughter must have carried to the party coming down the hillside, because now they heard a voice, still distant, but clear. "You down there. Where are you?"

"Sit up and tell them to come on down, can you?" said Gordon.

Roland answered and then retreated back under the blanket. It was still very cold, but there was more than warmth under the blanket, there was security. As he wriggled himself down Gordon said, "What did you tell them? Did you tell them I'd broken my leg?"

"I told them. I told them you'd need a stretcher."

"Thank God," said Gordon, and Roland knew then that all this time the leg had not ceased to hurt.

They could hear the footsteps now, and muttered voices. Every so often came the rattle of a stone and then, suddenly, the flash of a torch through the trees. It was only a matter of minutes, and Roland felt his stomach tighten. His increased tension must have communicated itself to Gordon because he said, "When they come, when they ask you questions, just tell the truth. Don't add anything you don't have to — one way or the other. If they're — if you think they're maybe a bit harsh with you, just put up with it, see? They mightn't let you stay with me."

"OK. Thanks. And —" He seemed to find it hard to go on, but presently he said, "Are you going to ask them about the baby? What happened?" It was a question that had become desperately important. There was no pushing it away now.

"They'll probably tell you. But if I can I'll ask when you're there to hear."

The footsteps were much nearer. The torch came bobbing down the track and they could count the number of men. There were three. Two things now became clear to Roland. One was the temporary calm, the companionship and the support, had come to an end. The other was that 'his cop' was going to be taken away from him. The sense of property that he had come to feel in the last twenty-four hours both for the dog that he had saved and for the cop that he had, he liked to think, saved, was both novel and powerful. But both would go their own ways, leaving him. He waited as the men came down the track. When they were near enough and the jerky light of the torch was almost above them, he shouted, "Here," and climbed carefully out from the blanket. He remembered not to bump his cop as he did so.

"Right." The torch wavered down into the little gully and picked them up, shining full in their faces. "We can see you now. Sutton, you OK?"

Before he could answer Roland said angrily, "What do you think? He's got a broken leg." And he would have elaborated if he had not heard Gordon's voice from beside his feet.

"Shut up, for God's sake." Then, more loudly, "OK as I can be. The kid's kept me warm." And Roland knew it was for his benefit the last statement had been added.

Chapter Thirteen

The three men climbed down. The torch flashed up and down Roland's half naked body and then on to Gordon lying under his pile of coats and rugs. One of the men was carrying a stretcher and another what looked like a pile of blankets. They laid them beside Gordon and one went down on his knees and said, "Right. Let's have a look at you." Roland stood apparently unnoticed as they peeled off the waterproof cape, the parka and the blanket. "Like unpeeling an onion," one of them said as the last covering came off. He put his hand on Gordon's chest. "Seem to be warm enough, anyway. That's a great thing. Now which leg is it?"

There was really no need to ask. The leg with its unnatural kink and the rough splint was plain enough. He began very gently to touch it. Gordon gasped. Roland jumped forward and pushed the man away so that he fell backwards. Immediately the two others closed in one each side of him, grabbed him none too gently by the arms and pulled him back. They continued to hold him between them while the one he had pushed over got to his feet and returned to his study of Gordon's leg.

"You do that once more," said the sergeant, "and you'll be in all sorts of trouble." He seemed to notice Roland's appearance for the first time, for he added, "Why are you naked, anyway? Where's your shirt?"

Before he could answer the ambulance man looking at Gordon's leg said, "I think it's round this sort of splint here. Looks like a shirt."

The sergeant gave his arm a shake. "That right?" When he nodded, the sergeant gave a grunt and said nothing more.

They stood in silence while the inspection went on. Once the ambulance man directing the torch on the leg slipped on the wet ground and said, "Sorry, mate." Once again Gordon made a small sound, but nothing more happened until the man working on the leg stepped back and said, "Don't think I'll do any more now. It's very swollen and I won't touch it. The sooner he's in hospital the better. Can you help me lift him on to the stretcher now?" He moved to Gordon's head. "We won't jolt you more than we can help, and I'll give you a painkiller now. It'll be a long way up the track."

Getting Gordon on to the stretcher was not easy, and in the end they allowed Roland to help. It was an agonising process for them all, knowing that Gordon was trying to keep quiet. In the end it was done and by the time it was over and in spite of the chill of the night air his face was glistening with sweat. As they covered him with the blanket Roland heard him say, "Let the kid put my parka on. He's perishing cold."

The sergeant, who was holding the coverings, did so, holding it out without a word and letting Roland slip his arms into it. It was far too big and his hands disappeared from sight, but it covered him half-way to the knees. With the extra warmth came very slightly a return of the courage he was needing. In the darkness the sergeant had not noticed the state of his back.

The painkiller was beginning to take effect, and Gordon said, with the strained note gone from his voice, "What's the news of the baby that — that was hit?"

The sergeant said, choosing his words, "If you mean is there a manslaughter charge added to this kid's lengthy list, no, there isn't."

By the time they had lifted him up to the track and prepared for the long climb upward there was no more need of the torch. The day had come and it was a clear day and before long the first long rays of the sun pierced through the tree trunks, flooding them with yellow light. All the birds in the valley left their perches of the night and flew, chirruping, squawking, gurgling, twittering, through the morning air in search of food.

When they reached the gate Roland found that Gordon, as he had warned, had left him. He was taking no more interest in Roland, or the coming of the day, for which, together they had waited so interminably, or anything at all. Roland could only be glad, but in the company of the three men, all of whom ignored him, he felt very lonely indeed.

Very slowly, with the stretcher bearers resting often, they climbed the hill. There was no question of Roland falling behind and slipping away into the scrub because he was never permitted to be the last in the procession. The sergeant always walked behind him. Even when he had to stop and retie his shoelace the sergeant waited until he was done and then came on behind him again. The men talked occasionally and he learned their names. The sergeant was Jack and the two ambulance men Lester and Syd. By the time they reached the gate Roland had them sorted out. He had a number of other things sorted out, too, and one was that now he seemed of little importance to any of them. He was of no importance at all any more to Gordon, and, after the unique experience of the last twenty-four hours, when everything Roland did, or decided, had been of supreme importance, it surprised him that the change — to what, in many ways was his normal state — could be so difficult and even painful to accept.

By the time they reached the gate the attempts at conversation of any kind had given way to concentrated heavy breathing. A lifetime, it seemed, had passed since Roland had found the dog hanging on the gate, and now the dog had gone as if it had never been, and for the three men with him it did not exist at all. Only Gordon knew and only Gordon would ever know what last night had meant. Perhaps he would be the only person ever to know what Roland was really like, and to understand what made him do the things he did. When they reached the road, that might be the last he would see of Gordon until, perhaps, in the witness box. Like the dog, he would be gone.

This time Roland was not even allowed to shut the gate. The sergeant did that, and he was told not to wait. But from time to time they all stopped to catch their breath. The stretcher could not be put down, but Lester and Syd would look and make comments.

"Colour all right, Lester?"

"Coming round, is he?"

But Roland was not given an opportunity to see. He found it strange that they ignored his existence so completely. They only spoke to him when it was necessary.

Considering that all of them, including Gordon, were here at all because of him it seemed very odd. But when, at long last, they reached the road in mid-afternoon, he learned the reason. As they were about to slide the stretcher into the ambulance Roland gathered his courage and went up to the sergeant.

"Could I — could I look at him, do you think, before they take him away?"

They stopped then and looked at him and he realised suddenly what had been in their minds all the time, why he had been treated as if he scarcely existed. The sergeant spelled it out for him. "I don't see why you should. If it hadn't been for you he wouldn't have broken his leg, would he? You think, do you, that because you did what you could afterwards, what any normal human being would have done, that it makes it OK, do you?" Roland stepped back then and stood in silence while they loaded the stretcher in, shut the doors and drove off. But he was still watching it grow smaller down the road when the sergeant said, "OK. Get in then. Your dad'll probably be waiting at the station."

"My dad? Why?" Suddenly, all over again, he was afraid.

"We had to let him know, didn't we? You're his responsibility. He'll have to sort you out — if that's possible."

He knew the last remark was unfair, but he had learned to do without fairness. He climbed into the back of the car and the sergeant threw the apricot-coloured blanket with the embroidered lamb in one corner on top of him. The pillow followed. Sitting there with these reminders of his last time in this same car he was filled with sadness. He found himself wishing he could turn back the clock, have only those last hours to remember, even if they had been anxious and filled with worry over the state of his cop. He had fitted into everything then and had been an important part of what happened. Now he was nothing. He was back where he started, not counting and, worse, he was heading back to face his father. He rubbed the sleeve of Gordon's parka angrily across his eyes.

At first he sat bolt upright and from the tumbled heap of the blanket the embroidered lamb gazed reproachfully up at him. He thought he would never sleep again, but the inside of the car was warm, and once they reached the highway it was no longer necessary to brace himself against sharp corners and bumps. Without warning a cloud of weariness came down and enveloped him and his muscles quite suddenly relaxed. He fell back and at once felt the pain of the cuts. He had not thought about his back for a long time and the pain of it now, coming on top of his shattered world, was the unkindest, the most unjust act of fate. Everything was against him, and his father waited at the end of the journey. He curled up on the seat and wished he was dead.

Chapter Fourteen

He had hoped the journey would never end, but it seemed to him that as soon as he had settled himself on the seat someone was putting a heavy hand on his back.

"Argh!" he shouted as he felt the pain and shrank away from the torturing hand. They must have imagined he had thoughts of escape, for they grabbed him now by the arm and he found himself pulled head first out of the open car door. He would have fallen, but he found himself dragged forward by a strong hand under each elbow and in this way taken into the police station.

"You're hurting me," he shouted as he came through the door — and found himself face to face with his father.

Mr Fleming seemed to fill the entire room. He was tall, broad-shouldered, none too slim, and he wore a heavy camel-hair overcoat that accentuated his girth. His face, now a darker shade of red than it usually was, flamed angrily beneath an incongruously gentle covering of fair, straight hair.

"Kindly let go my son," he roared, and they loosed their

hold so that Roland stumbled forward. But when he saw the hunched shoulders, the quivering knees and the pale, agonised face that looked up at him he seemed to become angrier still.

"Can't you stand a bit of manhandling? What's wrong with you? I was told it was the police officer who was hurt, not you."

Roland knew that anything he now said would enrage his father even more, so he said nothing. It was not until they took the parka off his back that the men standing behind him saw what state it was in. Without speaking, the sergeant turned him round so that his father could see the cuts on his back. They were an impressive sight, for the dried blood was smeared all over his back, one or two of them showed signs of bleeding again, and it was obvious that others had become infected. They looked as painful as they were. But if the sergeant was hoping to demonstrate that it was not police brutality but previous damage that he was complaining about he found he had made a mistake. Roland's father never defended where he could attack, and he saw his opportunity now.

"Do you mean to tell me you brought the boy all the way back in that condition? Didn't you even attempt to do something for him? I can see from here those cuts are poisoned and should have been treated. Why hasn't something been done?"

When he finally stopped to draw breath it was not the sergeant who answered him but, surprisingly, his own son. "They didn't know, Dad. I never told them. And, see, it was dark."

The remark hit his father like a bucket of cold water. For a moment he was off balance. And, Roland thought, a shadow of something that for once was not contempt seemed to cross his face. But he had no intention of losing the advantage he thought he had. "It's their job, surely, to look for this kind of thing. I can see exactly how it was. You were all so intent on looking after your own man it never even occurred to you to see to my son. It seems to me you quite obviously neglected your duty."

No one answered him. The formalities were gone through with the minimum of speech by the sergeant. Nevertheless, when he was charged and it was all completed and they were about to leave the station, Roland felt as he always did in the company of his father, that Mr Fleming had won the day. They were about to go through the door when the sergeant said, "You'd better take your boy to casualty before you go home to have that back looked at."

Mr Fleming turned quickly. "You think so? You think I'd let a sick boy like this sit up till God knows when waiting until it suits the doctor to come and look at him? He's going to bed — now. And that's where the doctor will see him." He went out on the last word and Roland followed.

Outside on the pavement Mr Fleming said, "Wait." He stopped, took off his coat and held it out for Roland to step into. "If you haven't any clothes you'd better put this on." By now Roland was almost asleep on his feet, but he was awake enough to note with surprise how gently his father put the coat over his shoulders. As he got into the car, trying not to trip over the tails of the coat, he thought foggily that it was strange how just now he seemed to be living in the clothes of men so much bigger than he was.

His father got in, closed the door and started the engine. Its quiet, powerful purr was the sound Roland always associated with his father's cars. He was borne off feeling more like a trophy of the chase than his father's wayward son. If he had been able to choose, he would have preferred the second.

He hardly remembered getting into bed. The last sound his tired brain recorded was his father's voice on the telephone. As usual, he was angry. As usual, he was bullying the person on the other end. After that, Roland slept.

When he woke next, the doctor was standing beside the bed. His father's voice was saying, "Turn over, Roland."

What the doctor did to him was momentarily painful, but in the end soothing. It became apparent that while he slept his father had been manoeuvring, perhaps this time with success, for he said to the doctor, "Those cuts are going to take a time to heal, aren't they? That boy's not going to be ready for the magistrate's court. You'll have to give me a certificate to say so, doctor."

The doctor, whom Roland knew slightly as a popular and patient man, said, "I can't do that, you know. Once the boy's had a good night's sleep and some food, the cuts won't stop him doing anything he feels he can."

Mr Fleming's reply was ominous. "I think I know my son better than you do, doctor. I'm telling you he won't be fit —"

Roland to his own surprise found himself saying, "I'm getting up anyway. I'm going to see Gordon."

His father suddenly shouted, "You'll do as I say."

He knew that his father would probably end up somehow getting him out of trouble. His father always did. It was a temptation once again to let the battle rage over his head. The price would be what it had always been: his father's opinion of him and his own opinion of himself would sink a little lower fairly painlessly. He happened to look up and caught the doctor's eye. It had a speculative, waiting look. He said suddenly, "How is Gordon?"

The question took the doctor by surprise, but, perhaps welcoming the interruption, he said, "He's OK now. It was a nasty break. It'll take some time."

"Can I see him?"

"No you cannot." It was his father who answered, and the sound of his voice rang round the room.

Instead of retreating into silence and obedience as he always did, Roland ignored his father and said quietly to the doctor, "Can I, Doctor?" The doctor made no attempt to shout down Mr Fleming. He simply nodded to Roland. He was still watching him closely. Roland looked at his father.

"You heard what I said." Mr Fleming spoke without heat, confident he would be obeyed.

For the first time his total self-confidence brought a reaction from Roland. "Yes. I'm sorry, Dad. I've got to go." He lay back and closed his eyes. "Tomorrow. Tomorrow I'll go. OK, Doctor?"

Mr Fleming now said very quietly, "And how do you think you're going to get there? Walk? It's ten miles. You can walk ten miles, can you?"

But Roland was sure of his ground now. "I can walk ten miles if I have to." It was much easier to defy his father now that his eyes were shut.

"You realise, don't you, that if you can turn up at the hospital tomorrow you can go to court, too? Once you do that, you're out of my hands." If it was a threat it misfired.

"I think it's time I was out of your hands, Dad."

Suddenly his father capitulated. He shrugged, and all he said was, "You young fool." But he said it in a tone Roland had not heard before and almost it was as if he had at last been given the key to the front door.

The doctor was packing up his bag. As he walked to the

door he said, "I'll tell Gordon to expect you then, shall I?"

"Yes, please."

The doctor left after a brief goodbye to Mr Fleming. If he thought there might be trouble he was mistaken. Mr Fleming had no more to say.

After that, Roland slept for twelve hours. When he woke he thought he would die of hunger, but Mrs Bates had foreseen this and at once brought him a meal that she called breakfast.

"Breakfast?" said Roland.

"Well, it may be midday but I'd say you were breaking a fast, wouldn't you?" And she went off chuckling.

After the meal and before he had time to get up, his father came in again. This time he was quite calm. It seemed he was now fully acquainted with the details of the Ferrari and was faced with another court case if he decided to ignore all the claims of the furious owner.

"I'm going to settle out of court," he told Roland. "I suppose I'll have to buy him a new Ferrari, but it'll be easiest in the long run." Strangely, his forebearance was harder to take than his usual bluster.

Roland could only say, "Thank you, Dad." He then said something he had never said before. "I'm sorry, Dad. I was mad to do it."

Chapter Fifteen

To his surprise Roland's father drove him to the hospital, and threatened to raise Cain if he were there longer than half an hour. "I've got some things to do, now I'm here. You be sure you're ready waiting on the step." He went off, but his face was its normal, slightly-veined pink.

It was the first time Roland had been inside a hospital, and he was nervous, frightened of the bustling nurses, and lost. Eventually one of them took pity on him and pointed out the door of Gordon's ward. Now that he was here and about to meet 'his cop' under such different circumstances he was not at all sure he wanted to. There would not be just the two of them as there had been before. There would be a whole ward full of people all looking and listening. And he would no longer be in control of the situation. Until now he had not realised how important this had been to him. But he was here and, in spite of it all, he knew that since it had all happened the one thing he wanted was to check on his cop again. He told himself it was to make sure they were looking after him properly. He wondered if he would recognise him, now that he would be just another face, clean and peering from between white sheets.

He need not have worried. The leg alone, hoisted in the air by a complicated arrangement of pulleys, would have told him. What made him immediately at ease, and justified his defiance of his father, was the delighted smile on Gordon's face immediately he saw Roland.

Gordon must have been visited already by the doctor, for the first words he said were, "So your Dad let you come."

Roland's smile seemed to take up the whole of his face. "Not really," he said.

Gordon made no comment. He only said, "I'm glad you came."

Now that he was here Roland found he had nothing to say. It was after a pause, while he waited for him to speak, that Gordon said, "The doctor tells me those are quite nasty cuts on your back. He said he'd have stitched you up if he'd seen you sooner."

"Glad he didn't, then," said Roland with such feeling that they both laughed, and the small tension was over.

Roland looked at the hoisted leg, and said, "Does it hurt?"

"It hurts," said Gordon. "Not all the time. Not as badly as it did before."

Roland looked at him closely. The face was shaved now and the eyes clear and intelligent. "I bet it hurt. You never looked like this down there."

"Didn't feel like this, come to that." Again they both laughed.

Gordon stopped laughing then and said, "You did a good job down there. Reckon I've got a lot to thank you for. I haven't yet, have I?"

Roland remembered the sergeant's words, spoken with such bitterness. "You don't have to," he said. "It was me got you there."

"I don't remember you made me fall on that stone that broke my leg. If you'd left me that night —" He turned his head to look at Roland. "You could have, you know. You nearly did, didn't you?"

Roland nodded. "Didn't have the nerve in the end. Dad says I don't have any guts."

"Matter of opinion. I think it took more guts to come back." He stopped and then said, "Mary wants to thank you, too."

"To *thank* me? Thought she'd want to kill me."

"There you are, you see. You never can tell, can you?"

They talked, relaxed and contented, until Gordon said, "Have you thought about the court case?" Roland nodded. "Know what it'll probably mean? I'm afraid they'll send you away somewhere."

"Dad reckons he'll get me off."

"Are you going to let him?"

It was the question Roland had been asking himself ever since he woke up. Now that Gordon asked it direct, and looked him full in the face as he did so, suddenly he knew the answer. "No," he said. Then he added, "Don't know what Dad'll say."

"Have you ever thought," Gordon began slowly, "have you ever thought maybe your dad'd be glad if you stood up to him now and then?"

"He never gave me a chance."

"Well try. Just once, try."

"If you say."

There was one more subject that came up before he left. Gordon said, "You never asked about the baby."

This time Roland seemed to be studying something that had fallen on the floor. "Wasn't game."

"I thought not. So I'll tell you. I asked Jack, the sergeant. He said the baby was shocked and bruised, and so was the mother shocked. But all the blankets it was wrapped in stopped any real damage. They were both in here for a couple of days afterwards. They're both OK now. But I think —" He stopped and looked carefully at Roland. "I think you ought to go and see her. Say you're sorry."

It was an appalling suggestion and Roland said, "She'll never want to see me."

"Maybe not. That's your problem. But *you* ought to see *her*. Will you?"

Roland said in a kind of wail, "You're worse than Dad." Gordon's laugh forced him to smile. "Oh — OK, if you think I should." A happy thought occurred to him. "But I don't know where she lives, even."

"Of course you don't. But I do. And I've got it here, written down for you."

Roland wondered as he left the ward if he would ever see his cop again. He knew that from now on his own actions would be dictated, not by himself, but by processes far beyond his and — he now hoped — his father's influence.

It was the same with the dog. He never knew the dog's name, and he never expected to see it again. Somehow it seemed to matter more that he never knew its name. He might not even recognise it if he saw it. He began to school himself into accepting what seemed to be inevitable.

But the one thing he was able to do of his own free will was to call on the mother of the baby. He had been prepared for anything and he was surprised that she greeted him with charity and even kindness. If she guessed what it had meant for him to visit her she did not let him know. But she brought the baby for him to see and, looking at it, he knew that for the first time it was not for himself he was glad it had not been damaged. He did not know if it was a boy or a girl and he did not like to ask, but whichever it was, it was alive.

He looked at her then and said, "Thank you", and he did not quite know what he was thanking her for. But she seemed to know, and she knew, too, that he was indeed thankful, even if it was not to her.

Chapter Sixteen

There was a week to wait until the magistrate's court. Mr Fleming said he could not stay out in the sticks, kicking his heels, and took Roland back to Sydney. It was a week that Roland never forgot, yet could never clearly remember. He was not confined to the house. He could go where he liked when he liked. The school term had started again and his friends had gone back to school. Most of them boarded as he did. Even if he could have seen them he did not want to. He thought of them now as strangers. For that week he did not leave the house, and his mother, rushing in between meetings, or saying good night to him when she came in, studied his face with her usual slightly embarrassing gaze and said, "You're not a prisoner, you know. And you're not the only person this has happened to. I'm not blaming you, except for being stupid. Even that's forgiveable, I suppose, in a boy of sixteen. Go out and try to live normally." But he could not. He lived most of the time in the immediate past, either carrying the dog or trying to keep his cop warm. The present — the comfortable present — scarcely existed for him.

His father never spoke of the court case, but he suspected that he was somehow actively preparing for it just the same. He did not really care. He knew now what he was going to do and he did not think it would be in his father's power to prevent him, once he made his wishes plain to everyone. It was clear his father was to be present in court. His mother gave no sign of her intentions. She continued to lead her active, absorbed life, though he began to wonder if there was the smallest hint of a question now in her good night gaze. But she said nothing, and he assumed he had imagined the question. As the days went by, he began to realise he was waiting for her to speak. He knew then that, more than anything else, he wanted her with him during the court case.

It was the final day before they were to leave Sydney, and he knew he had left it too late. But she came home early that night, and, because his father was out and they were alone, he said gruffly, revealing the effort it was costing him, "I wish you'd come with us tomorrow."

To his surprise, her expression changed at once and became softer, warmer than he had ever seen it. She made a sudden move towards him, but pulled herself up short, and her face resumed its normal brisk, confident expression. "Of course I'll come," she said. "Of course I will. I was only waiting —" Again she pulled herself up short.

"Your appointments —?" he said — and stopped.

"They're easily dealt with." And to his astonishment she left the room at once and from the distance he heard her voice on the telephone, authoritative and calm, cancelling one commitment after another. When she returned, she surprised him again. It seemed that for once she was at a loss for words. She gave a little, embarrassed laugh, reached out and pulled him to his feet.

"If we are to make an early start tomorrow we must go to bed," and he felt her arm lightly round his shoulders as she propelled him through the door. In spite of the coming ordeal, he slept a dreamless sleep that night. Next morning, his father's only comment was, "I suppose you've considered what this might do to your reputation on all those committees of yours?" She only laughed, but the comment depressed him. Perhaps it was something like this that was the motive behind his father's activities on his behalf — an attempt to protect his own reputation. Although he had not wanted his father to interfere, it was a thought he did not care for.

"It won't even be a nine days' wonder," his mother said easily. "This sort of thing happens every day."

"But not every silly boy has to hit a perambulator," his father said, suddenly angry. "Heavens above, surely you could have avoided that? It's big enough. That's what makes it difficult."

Roland and his father scarcely spoke at all on the morning of the court case. At breakfast only his mother appeared at ease. She spoke when necessary, but made no attempt at conversation. Once or twice she looked across the table at him, to give a brief smile and nod, and his pulse would slow and somewhere inside him a muscle would relax.

They all drove into town in silence, and in silence entered the court room. For Roland, it was alarming enough, but he was glad to see that there was no one in the court room but the magistrate, himself and his parents, and the police, whose faces he recognised. He did not see Gordon there and had not expected to. What his father had not taken into account was that he, himself, was news. One or two reporters were there trying to persuade him to answer questions, so that his attitude was belligerent from the beginning.

It seemed to Roland afterwards that all the talk had washed over his head. A lot of the procedure was vaguely familiar to him from his watching of television dramas. The police made statements, he was asked questions which he tried to answer truthfully, and his father, it seemed to him, talked a lot, and for the most part angrily. At the end the magistrate read from two papers.

Neither of these washed over his head. He found himself unwillingly attending. The first paper was apparently a statement written by Gordon from the hospital and the second, one that his father had submitted. Gordon's was a statement of his pursuit of Roland, ending, Roland was surprised to hear, with a comment on his own fortitude and resourcefulness after Gordon had broken his leg. His father's confined itself to quoting (or perhaps enclosing) a letter from an eminent specialist, whom Roland remembered as a friend of his father's, stating that Roland as a small child had been subject to — something with a long name — and therefore not always responsible for his actions. This, it seemed, had been the best his father could do — and not bad, Roland thought to himself, in that if it were true, no slur could be attached to Mr Fleming. Any child might be subject to whatever nasty disease was meant by the long Latin name. Roland could not, himself, recall it in his childhood.

He looked at his mother. Her eyes were wide and amazed and fixed on Mr Fleming. Her mouth was half open. For a moment he thought she was going to interrupt. He saw her move in her chair as if she was about to stand. Then her mouth closed and she sank back. But she was alert now to everything his father was saying. The magistrate now commented that the one paper appeared to cancel out the other. Resourcefulness and good sense seemed to him not to be consistent with the total lack of responsibility suggested by Mr Fleming's statement, and both, in this case, could not be right.

It was at this point that Mr Fleming got to his feet and delivered a telling and angry speech on his son's handicaps and shortcomings, all commands rather than pleas for leniency. There was a silence when he had finished, and for the first time Roland came to full awareness of exactly what was going on. He did not care at all for his father's efforts to turn him into an idiot. For the first time he took in the whole significance of where he was and why he was here.

When the magistrate allowed him to, he got up and faced his father. He spoke to the magistrate, but he continued to look directly at his father. "There has been a mistake. I did not have the disease, whatever its name was, that my father said. I remember the time perfectly well, and my father and the doctor must have forgotten. I had scarlet fever, and though I remember Mum saying I was delirious for a few days, I wasn't very ill." Here Mr Fleming made a sound in his throat and began to get up. But the magistrate held up his hand.

"Please, Mr Fleming. I want your son to continue."

When he was seated, Roland spoke again. "I can see quite well that my father is trying to get me off the hook. I'm grateful. But I resent the way he does it. I don't care to be made out more of a fool than I am." He swallowed. Never in his life had he felt like this — keyed up, furious, determined. It was not a bad feeling at all. He glanced at his mother. She was looking at him as if she shared his elation, as if for the first time she could be proud of him. "I'm not weak in the head, as my father seems to be trying to tell you. In fact, I'm quite bright. Perhaps I'm weak in other ways. Perhaps he's right. But I'm sick of being treated as if I were a silly child. I'm not. I'm not silly and I'm no longer a child. I'm sorry my father had to tell lies on my behalf. From now on, I'm prepared to answer for my own actions."

He was standing very straight. He stopped and looked again at his mother. He saw that now she was standing too, her hands clutching the back of the chair in front. Her expression was intent — almost as if she had stopped breathing. But when she saw him look at her it changed suddenly, and across the court she smiled at him — as clear a message as if she had shouted BRAVO.

He turned to face his father. Mr Fleming had only just begun to speak. If anyone had expected an outburst they were disappointed. His voice was quiet, and coming from somewhere deep inside him. Only Roland and his mother could detect the slight quiver beneath the measured words. He chose to speak directly to the magistrate. "I should like my son to consider very carefully what he is saying. I want him to search his memory again most carefully. I wish him to consider whose memory is most likely to be accurate — that of a fevered child, or of a mature, caring, not unintelligent adult."

"Well?" said the magistrate, and looked at Roland.

It was Mrs Fleming who answered. "My son's memory is correct. He had a mild attack of scarlet fever." And at last she sat down.

Roland spoke to his father. "I'm sorry, Dad. This is one time I won't be protected. I don't want to be shielded any longer. If I'd known this was what you were going to do for me I'd have asked you not to. I know what I did, and I know why I did it. You're right. I was a fool, as well as everything else. But this time I don't want to get out of it. Whatever happens now, I want it to be because of what I did, not because of what you did for me." Now he turned to face the magistrate. "I did it. All of it was my fault." He sat down and found he was trembling from head to foot. But the feeling that had made him speak still buoyed him up. Somehow he felt as if he were in control of the court. The magistrate would now have to act according to his statement. Knowing what he had brought on himself, his confidence still remained. He was not sorry, and, thinking of Gordon, he knew he was right. This time, and for once, it was his father who was wrong.

He walked out of the court, knowing his penalty, and he had no trouble meeting the gaze of the police, his father and the magistrate himself. At the end, his father had withdrawn his evidence, if it could now be called that. The specialist's report was torn up in view of the court, and if there was a defeat that day in that court, it was not Roland's.

Afterwards Roland remembered only one small exchange of speech. He found himself standing between his parents on the steps outside the court house. His mother had said, "I'm sorry, Hubert. This is one occasion he had to have support."

And Mr Fleming had turned to look at her. "I have been supporting him all his life." He had spoken, not angrily, but as if he were deeply puzzled.

Suddenly, not knowing then, or later, why he did it, Roland had put a hand on his father's arm and said, "Dad —" But when his father turned again he had nothing to say.

It seemed to have been enough. Mr Fleming's expression changed in a way it had never done before and he said, "Why should I suddenly feel proud of you, when you've done the most damned silly thing you've ever done in your life?"

Epilogue

He was sent for two years to one of the State's reform schools. He often suspected that his time there was made easier because of the plea for clemency in Gordon's statement. He was not able to see Gordon again, but later he wrote care of the local police station to thank him. During the two years, and mainly in the early days, he received several letters from Gordon, and replied to them all. His father wrote regularly. In not one of his letters did he refer to the past. If the letters were, on the whole, noncommittal, they were always friendly and at times as if his father were writing to an equal. His mother wrote often and warmly. He looked forward to her letters, but he wondered if the house in Sydney would ever seem like home again.

The two years came to an end. If his father was disappointed that he did not want to study for a profession he did not say so, but suggested instead that he might like to take over the farm. But Roland knew exactly what he wanted now, and thanked his father, saying he would try to find himself a job on his own.

Above all he wanted independence. His distant dream was to have a property of his own. He was confident that somehow, sooner or later, he could make the dream a reality. But he went back to the farm briefly. He had faced Mrs Bates, who still looked after the homestead, and anyone he might meet in the town who still remembered who he was. He did not find it particularly easy, but it was not as bad as he had thought it might be. It was all so far away, and from the distance of those two years at the reform school he looked back at himself as he might have looked at any other unreliable youth of sixteen.

He went to the police station, and one or two of them remembered him and were polite. But Gordon had left, and he recalled that the last letter, now about twelve months old, had said he was to be transferred. They told Roland the name of the town, but it was a long way away. He was sorry, but not too sorry. He was glad enough to have done with the past.

As it turned out, the whole episode, which he had hoped buried for good, was not quite dead. He was walking in the main street of the town one day, passing a parked utility truck muddy enough to have come from some outlying farm. A man was about to step into the driving seat. He had seen the man and the muddy utility before. It was, after all, a small town and farmers tended to frequent the same stores and agencies. This time he vaguely noticed there was a dog in the back. As he passed, a kind of whirlwind hurled itself from the utility and landed at his feet.

At the same time the man stepping into the truck began to shout. He seemed to be calling the dog. "Blue! Here, Blue," and shouted a warning to Roland at the same time. "Careful. He bites."

But the dog did not bite. It flung itself at Roland, jumping up and thumping him with its front paws and at the same time making small whimpering noises.

It was a few minutes before Roland realised what was happening. When he did, he bent down, picked up the dog and replaced it in the truck. He put his hand on its head and it did its best to lick his face. He was smiling. The owner came round and seemed inclined to hit the dog.

"It's all right," said Roland. "I think it remembered me. Can you tie it in so it doesn't try to follow me?" He gave it a final pat on the head and walked on quickly to avoid the questions obviously forming in the man's mind. He was glad to know the dog's name at last. He might have guessed it would be Blue.

You can see more titles in
Methuen Teens on the
following pages:

ANTHONY MASTERS

Streetwise

Sam's father, a policeman, has been killed. Driven
to find out the facts behind the death for himself, Sam
makes two important discoveries. His father had ruth-
less enemies – and he was leading a kind of double life.

Caught up in a dangerous chain of events, Sam
undergoes a powerful and shocking voyage of dis-
covery . . .

JUDITH ST GEORGE

You've Got To Believe Me

Matt wished he'd never moved to Cape Cod. The cold ocean winds and the bleakness of the winter salt marsh were not at all to his liking, and neither were the Cape Codders – especially ecology-spouting Julie Chamberlain. Then there was Bluff Cottage. Something very strange was happening there, and it looked as if Matt was being drawn into trouble.

Matt reported a break-in at the cottage, but no-one believed him. He went in search of Julie and then the violence erupted . . .

WILLIAM SLEATOR

Interstellar Pig

Barney is excited by rumours of ghosts in the rented
summer house – and then the new neighbours arrive.
They seem friendly enough, and even invite Barney to
play their unusual board game, Interstellar Pig.

But are the strangers what they seem? Is the board
game just a new and sophisticated entertainment – or
something more sinister? Why are the newcomers so
anxious to see inside Barney's house? And what is the
significance of the pink, smiling Piggy . . . that has to
be won at all costs?

Barney is drawn deeper and deeper into the compul-
sive game until the terrifying truth is revealed . . .

JUDITH ST GEORGE

HAUNTED

Alex didn't like the place from the moment he arrived. It made him shiver as he remembered that the previous owner had shot and killed himself and his wife.

Strange things begin to happen. A friendly dog goes berserk and tries to kill him. He's sure that he sees a pale face at the window, and feels someone needs his help. But someone is determined that he shan't give it. Alex finds himself sucked into an uncontrollable situation. Could it have something to do with the dead man's Nazi past? He just has to find out, however terrifying the experience may be . . .

MICHAEL MORPURGO

Why The Whales Came

"You keep away from the Birdman," warned Gracie's father. "Keep well clear of him, do you hear?"

But Gracie and her friend Daniel discover that the Birdman isn't mad or dangerous as everyone says. Yet he does warn them to stay away from the abandoned Samson Island – he says it's cursed. And when the children are stranded on Samson by fog, Gracie returns home to hear of a tragic death. Could the Birdman be right?

On the day the whale is found stranded on the beach, the Birdman is forced to reveal his secret – or the cycle of disaster will begin all over again . . .

"An adventure story with a tantalizing mystery at its centre . . . rich, complex and thought-provoking"
Times Literary Supplement

BARBARA AND SCOTT SIEGEL

FIREBRATS 1

The Burning Land

Matt and Dani scarcely know one another when the
unthinkable happened. World War 3. Thrown together
in a theatre basement, living on junk food, they were
desperate to get out . . . But was there anyone out
there to help them?

An exciting adventure story of two teenagers strug-
gling to survive in the horrors of a nuclear-bombed city,
where everything they know has been destroyed . . .

While every effort is made to keep prices low, it is sometimes necessary to increase prices at short notice. Magnet books reserve the right to show new retail prices on covers which may differ from those previously advertised in the text or elsewhere.

The prices shown below were correct at the time of going to press.

☐	416 06252 0	Nick's October	*Alison Prince*	£1.95
☐	416 08822 8	The Changeover	*Margaret Mahy*	£1.95
☐	416 11962 X	The Teens Book of Love Stories	*ed. M Hodgson*	£1.95
☐	416 07422 7	Taking Terri Mueller	*Norma Fox Mazer*	£1.95
☐	416 10242 5	Don't Blame the Music	*Caroline Cooney*	£1.95
☐	416 08662 4	Over the Moon	*E Haden Guest*	£1.95
☐	416 10252 2	The Doom of Soulis	*Moira Miller*	£1.95
☐	416 09812 6	Interstellar Pig	*William Sleator*	£1.95
☐	416 06232 6	Haunted	*Judith St George*	£1.95
☐	416 07442 1	Howl's Moving Castle	*Diana Wynne Jones*	£1.95
☐	416 09242 X	Monsterman	*J & D Eldridge*	£1.95
☐	416 10172 0	Groosham Grange	*Anthony Horowitz*	£1.95
☐	416 03202 8	The Burning Land	*B & S Siegel*	£1.95
☐	416 03192 7	Survivors	*B & S Siegel*	£1.95
☐	416 09232 2	Short Cut to Love	*Mary Hooper*	£1.99
☐	416 04022 5	Fire And Hemlock	*Diana Wynne Jones*	£1.95

All these books are available at your bookshop or newsagent, or can be ordered direct from the publisher. Just tick the titles you want and fill in the form below.

METHUEN BOOKS Cash Sales Department
P.O. Box 11, Falmouth,
Cornwall TR10 9EN

Please send cheque or postal order, no currency, for purchaser price quoted and allow the following for postage and packing;

UK	60p for the first book, 25p for the second book and 15p for each additional book ordered to a maximum charge of £1.90.
BFPO and Eire	60p for the first book, 25p for the second book and 15p for each next seven books, thereafter 9p per book.
Overseas Customers	£1.25 for the first book, 75p for the second book and 28p for each subsequent title ordered.

NAME (Block letters) ....

ADDRESS ....

....